IN FROM THE COLD: The I Spy Stories

Josh Lanyon

IN FROM THE COLD: THE I SPY STORIES

Cover Art by KB Smith
Cover photos by Coka and DrunkDwarf licensed through Shutterstock.

ISBN: 978-1-937909-35-2

Printed in the United States of America

Just Joshin'
3053 Rancho Vista Blvd.
Suite 116
Palmdale, CA 93551
www.joshlanyon.com

Table of Contents

I SPY SOMETHING BLOODY

Josh Lanyon

Chapter One

The telephone rang and rang. I stared through the window glass of the phone box at rugged green moorland and the distant snaggletoothed remains of a prehistoric circle. The rolling open hills of Devon looked blue and barren against the rain-washed sky. I'd read somewhere they'd filmed *The Hound of the Baskervilles* around here. It looked like a good day for a hellhound to be out and about, prowling the eerie ruins and chasing virgin squeak toys to their deaths.

To the north were the military firing zones, silent this afternoon.

The phone continued to ring—a faraway jangle on the other end of the line.

I closed my eyes for a moment. It felt years since I'd really slept. The glass was cool against my forehead. Why had I come back? What had I hoped to accomplish? It wasn't as though Barry Shelton and I had been best mates. He'd been a colleague. Quiet, tough, capable. I'd known a lot of Barry Sheltons through the years. Their faces all ran together. Just another anonymous young man—like me.

He died for nothing. A pointless, stupid, violent death. For nothing!

I could still hear Shelton's mother screaming at me, blaming me. Why not? It was as much my fault as anyone's. It didn't matter. I wasn't exactly the sensitive type. Neither had been Shelton. The only puzzle was why I'd imagined the news would come better from me. Wasn't even my style, really, dropping in on the widows and orphans and Aged Ps. That kind of thing was much better handled by the Old Man.

My leg was aching. And my ribs. Rain ticked against the glass. I opened my eyes. The wet-dark road was wide and empty. I could see miles in either direction. All clear. The wind whistled forlornly through the places where the door didn't join snugly; a mournful tune like a melody played on the *tula*.

Unexpectedly, the receiver was picked up. A deep voice—with just that hint of Virginia accent—said against my ear, "Stephen Thorpe."

I hadn't expected to be so moved by just the sound of his voice. Funny really, although laughter was the furthest thing from me. My throat closed and I had to work to get anything out.

"It's Mark," I managed huskily, after too long a pause.

Silence.

He was there, though. I could hear the live and open stillness on the other end of the line. "Stephen?" I said.

"What did you want, Mark?" he asked quietly. Too quietly.

"I'm in trouble." It was a mistake. I knew that the instant I said it. I should be apologizing, wooing him, not begging for help, not compounding my many errors. My hand clenched the receiver so hard my fingers felt numb. "Stephen?"

"I'm listening."

"Can I come home?"

He said without anger, "This isn't your home."

My heart pounded so hard I could hardly hear over the hollow thud. My mouth felt gummy-dry, the way it used to before an op. A long time ago. I licked my lips. No point arguing now. No time. I said, "I…don't have anywhere else to go."

Not his problem. I could hear him thinking it. And quite rightly.

He said with slow finality, "I don't think that coming here would be a good idea, Mark."

I didn't blame him. And I wasn't surprised. Not really. But surprised or not, it hurt like hell. More than I expected. I'd been prepared to play desperate; it was a little shock to realize I didn't have to play. My voice shook as I said, "Please, Stephen. I wouldn't ask if it—please."

Nothing but the crackling emptiness of the open line. I feared he would hang up, that this tenuous connection would be lost—and then I would be lost. Stranded here at the ends of the Earth where bleak sky fused into wind-scoured wilderness.

Where the only person I knew was Barry Shelton's mother.

I opened my mouth—Stephen had once said I could talk him into anything—but I was out of arguments. Too tired to make them even if I'd known the magic words. All that came out was a long, shuddering sigh.

I don't know if Stephen heard it all the way across the Atlantic, but after another heartbeat he said abruptly, "All right then. Come."

I replaced the receiver very carefully and pushed open the door. The wind was cold against my face, laced with rain. Rain and a hint of the distant sea; I could taste the salty wet on my lips.

* * * * *

The flight from Heathrow to Dulles took eight hours. Eight hours through the stars and the clouds. Between my ribs and my leg, sleep was impossible—even if I'd felt safe enough to take a couple of painkillers and shut off. I tried reading a few pages of Dickens' *Little Dorrit,* then settled for numbing myself with alcohol and staring out the window. I don't remember thinking much of anything; I barely remember the flight. I just remember hurting and welcoming the hurt because it would keep me sharp. Which was proof of how drunk I was.

I waited longer for my connecting plane to Virginia than the flight itself took. By then I was sobering up, and my various aches and pains were fast reaching the point where I wanted to murder the bloke coughing incessantly behind me—and the baby screaming in front. I wasn't crazy about any of the other passengers either. Or the flight crew. Or the ground crew. Or anyone else on the ground. Or in the air. Or on the planet. Or in the solar system.

I tried to think happy thoughts, but happy thoughts weren't a big part of my job description. So I thought unhappy thoughts about

Stephen not wanting me to come back. “This isn’t your home,” he’d said, and so much for Southern hospitality.

I waited my whole life for you. I can wait a few months more…

Time flies when you’re having fun, I suppose.

Was it that easy for him to turn it off? Because I’d tried and I couldn’t do it. If anything, my need for Stephen grew stronger with each passing day. It would be convenient to be able to turn off the memories: the way his green eyes crinkled at the corner when he smiled that slow, sexy grin; the way his damp hair smelled right out of the shower—a blend of orange and bamboo and vetiver that always inexplicably reminded me of the old open air market in Bengal; the way that soft Southern drawl got a little more pronounced when he was sleepy—or when we made love. Yeah, made love. It hadn’t just been fucking. Stephen had loved me. I was sure of it.

He’d said so. And I didn’t think he’d lie about it. Like it said in *Little Dorrit*, “Once a gentleman, and always a gentleman.”

I was the liar. But I’d said the words too. And meant them.

* * * * *

We landed at Shenandoah Valley Airport just after eleven o’clock in the morning, and I stumbled off the plane, exhausted and edgy, tensing as hurrying passengers brushed past, crowding me. Too many people—and everyone’s voice sounded harsh, too loud, nearly sending me out of my skin.

After what felt like several nerve-wrenching miles of this, Stephen appeared out of nowhere, striding towards me in that loose, easy way. I had never seen anything more beautiful. Tall and lean, broad shoulders and long legs, hair prematurely silver—striking with his youthful face. He was fifty now. I had missed his birthday. Missed it by a month. By a mile. Just one of many things I'd missed.

At the sight of me, he checked midstride, then came forward.

"What the hell happened to you?"

I offered a smile—to which he did not respond. "Long story."

There were tiny lines around his eyes that I didn't remember before—a sternness to his mouth that was new.

"Another one?" The tone was dry, but his expression gave me a little hope.

I hadn't realized how much I missed him till he was standing arm's length from me, and then it was like physical pain: He was so familiar, so…dear—like a glimpse of land after months at sea. The boyishly ruffled pale hair, the spring green of his eyes…

I thought for an instant he might even take me into his arms, but no. Instead he took my bag, took my elbow, took charge. His fingers were warm—if a little steely—wrapping around my arm. And although it was not exactly what I wanted, it was a relief. A welcome relief to rely on someone else—to rely on Stephen. There was no one else in the world I trusted. Not even the Old Man. Not anymore. Only Stephen.

The feeling no longer appeared to be mutual.

"We'll have to hurry," he said crisply. "I'm on call." And he glanced automatically at his wristwatch. The watch I had given him on the one birthday I'd been around for. An artifact of a relationship lost to time and distance; there seemed something ironic in my choice now.

"You needn't have come yourself," I said, hobbling along. "I could have grabbed a cab."

Wrong answer again. He gave me an austere look, his hand tightening wardenlike on my bicep, unconsciously lengthening his stride. He must have talked to one of his mates in the Justice Department. I hadn't expected him at the airport, and hadn't offered any flight info.

Sweat broke out along my back, my underarms. It was oppressively hot in the airport terminal—or maybe it was just me. Stephen looked as cool and poised as a marble statue in a crystal fountain—if marble statues wore jeans and black polo shirts. His profile was impassive as he steered me along, impersonal and efficient. Overhead the loudspeaker announced another arrival—or perhaps another departure. It was all starting to run together.

We stepped outside and the late May sun blasted down, shimmering off the pavement in waves. I swayed a little and Stephen's arm came around my waist, hard and reassuring.

"All right?"

I offered a crooked grin. "A bit tired…"

"The Jeep's just over here."

The "Jeep," which was in fact a black SUV, was parked in one of the lots adjacent to the general aviation terminal. The smell of asphalt and jet engine exhaust hung in the still, humid air as we walked across the parking lot.

Stephen unlocked the front passenger door, tossed my holdall into the rear seat, and helped me up. I dropped back in the seat and wiped my forehead.

He lowered the window a few centimeters. "Sit tight." The door slammed shut; Stephen locked me in using the remote key fob and was gone before I got myself together enough to tell him I didn't have any luggage.

I sat there, head back, feeling woozy with heat and exhaustion—the dregs of alcohol moving sluggishly through my bloodstream. I stared up through the twin sunroof windows at the unmoving clouds in the blue sky. Blue as water. Deep water. For an instant I had the sensation of falling forward into it.

I shook my head, reached back for my holdall. Unzipping it, I fished out the steel and polymer pieces of my Glock 18, assembling them quickly. The grip felt right in my hand. Familiar. Reassuring. I slapped the magazine in.

Untrue about the Glock not setting off airport metal detectors. The metal barrel, slide, magazine—not to mention the ammo—could all be detected by X-ray machines. But my employers had a certain…licensing agreement with the U.S. Government. And I'd taken advantage of that. These days I never traveled unarmed. Not that I was expecting trouble. No more than usual.

I let my head fall back again, pistol resting in my lap. Closed my eyes telling myself it would just be for a moment. Just to rest my eyes. Christ, I was so…*tired*…

The sound of the automatic locks flicking over jerked me awake. The door opened and I lunged across the console and shoved my pistol in Stephen's face before I realized it *was* Stephen.

"Jesus Christ! Are you *crazy*?" he said furiously, even as I brought the pistol down.

A legitimate question. I wasn't sure myself of the answer anymore. He was staring at me like I was from another planet.

"Sorry," I got out. "Stephen, I'm…sorry. You startled me."

"It's mutual." He got in, slammed the door with barely restrained violence. He rested his hands on the steering wheel, not looking at me. "Maybe you'd better tell me what's going on."

A right rollicking cock-up from first to last, Mr. Hardwicke.

I'm sorry, sir.

Sorry? Sorry is for lovers and politicians. If the press gets wind of this…

"Can we have…the air?" I requested. I mopped my face with my sleeve. It was stifling—impossible to breathe in the close confines of the vehicle.

He did look at me then. A hard long look. He turned the key and cold air blasted out of the dashboard vents; it steadied me like a slap. I took a couple of deep breaths. ICBM. Instant Calm Breath Method. And I was okay again.

I realized that Stephen had made no move to start driving —was waiting for me to talk.

I wondered if he'd do it. If he was angry enough, disgusted enough to shove me out of the car and leave me. I found the idea funny, and I knew I had a weird smile on my face—could tell by the way his brows drew together. I said, "There's not a lot to tell, really. The job…went south. I had some leave coming…"

"And you wanted to spend it here? I'm honored." He didn't sound honored. He sounded acrid.

I wasn't sure what to say. That last had clearly been wrong—giving no clue to how much I'd missed him, how much I wanted to make it all up to him. I was so bad at this kind of thing. Always. Until Stephen made it easy. Probably because he had done all the work.

My vision blurred, and I rubbed my eyes, trying to focus on his face. But Stephen's profile didn't encourage further heartfelt confidences. He started the engine.

We pulled out of the airport car park without further discussion. I thought of the pain pills in my bag, decided they weren't worth the bother.

Stephen expertly negotiated the SUV's passage through pedestrians and other vehicles. Before long we were on the main motorway, picking up speed. I relaxed a fraction.

Signs flashed by, offering information, urging caution, spelling out the rules. So many rules in a civilized society. How did people remember them all? So many things to be careful of, cautious of.

Stephen turned on the radio.

"...stated in a press briefing, "U.S. and coalition forces operating in Afghanistan are to continue to have the freedom of action required to conduct appropriate military operations based on consultations and pre-agreed procedures..."

He changed the channel, sliding through talk radio, adverts, static, and settling at last on a classical music station. Ballade no. 1 in G Minor.

I realized I'd been holding my breath, and I exhaled softly. Focused on the scenery sailing past. I'd forgotten how pretty it was here. "Daughter of the Stars," that was what the Indian word *Shenandoah* was supposed to mean. It was one of the loveliest places I'd ever been. Green as England, but a nicer climate. I remembered cool, crisp mornings and lazy, sunny afternoons—and the stars at night. A sky full of stars glittering like diamond dust. I had left before the first snowfall, but I could imagine how pretty it was in the winter. Like an old-fashioned greeting card. There were a lot of farms here, and we wove our way through a patchwork quilt of gold fields and green orchards.

To the east were the Blue Ridge Mountains, to the west, the Appalachians, and through the rich and fertile valley, the famous river itself glinted and tumbled along its rolling way. Compared to the ancient worm-holed history of Afghanistan, this part of the world seemed relatively young and untouched. But that was an illusion. The American War of Independence, the War Between the States—the valley had been a strategic target for both the South and North.

Most of Stephen's family had fought for the Confederacy—and their fortunes had fallen with it. But they had been lucky. The Thorpes had Northern relations and loyal, influential friends; picking up the pieces after the war had been easier for them than for most. The family had recovered its fortune within a generation. Now Stephen belonged to a committee dedicated to preserving Civil War battlefields in the Shenandoah Valley.

"What's wrong with your leg?"

I forced my attention back on Stephen. "Nothing really."

"Were you knifed or shot?" He sounded angry again.

I said vaguely. "A screwdriver, actually." Then, at the tension in his face, "Don't ask if you don't want to know."

"Has anyone looked at it?"

"Countless people. It was quite the topic of conversation on the plane."

He was unamused.

"It's fine," I reassured. "It's healing." It had stopped bleeding at least. I'd changed jeans on the airbus. I'd had to run to make the flight, and the wound had come open again. Stressful for the other passengers but nothing serious. I needed new stitches, but that was nothing that would keep me out of action for long. Not that I wouldn't have liked to play doctor with Stephen.

"That's right," he said. "You're a valuable commodity. Your employer will want you fighting fit again as soon as possible."

"Asset is the word you're looking for," I said.

"Is it?"

I hated that cool tone. I hated the fact that he didn't look at me. I realized for the first time that coming back here might have been a mistake. A worse mistake than leaving.

I said, half-joking—trying to sound like I was joking anyway, "Still. Good to know someone cares if I live or die."

"I don't want you dead, Mark," Stephen said. "I just want you out of my life." He didn't smile. I felt my own fading.

I gazed out the window at the fields of a vineyard. Rows and rows of green leaves glistening in the sun. An occasional billboard flew by. After a time I put my head back and slept.

Chapter Two

"We're home."

The words sounded hard, unwelcoming.

I opened my eyes. Stephen had the car door open and stood beside it, holding my bag.

I blinked at him, wiped my bleary eyes. "You what?"

"We're at the house."

"Right. Yes." Still half-asleep, I fumbled around with the seatbelt and then unfolded awkwardly from the car, reaching for the door to steady myself.

We were parked in the shady circular drive in front of a white mansion. Built back in the 1800s, the house was a blend of traditional Queen Anne architecture and stone and shingled New England cottage. Pretty. Prettier than I remembered. Inside it had high ceilings and hardwood floors and a lot of antique furniture. I recalled the huge old bed I'd shared with Stephen, the moonlit nights and the sound of the geese down by the lake, and lazy, sunny mornings with breakfast in bed—not that I recollected eating a lot of breakfast. Truthfully, I didn't remember much about the house—never thought of it really, beyond being where I could find Stephen. I realized now that it was lovely. And, unexpectedly, it looked like home.

My leg was stiff and uncooperative after the long drive; I staggered a little as I stepped away from the car. Stephen moved to steady me—reluctantly. I could feel that reluctance to touch me as though he'd said it aloud, and it hurt worse than my leg.

Strange, because his arm felt so familiar against my back. It was like my bones and muscles recognized his touch. I didn't understand how it could feel so right to me, but not to Stephen. I wanted to ask him about that, but it was hard to think of how to put it without further offending him. And yet he used to be the easiest person in the world to talk to. There was a time when I'd thought I could tell him anything.

"All right?" he asked.

I nodded vaguely, looking toward the house as a large chocolate-brown dog, a Chesapeake Bay retriever, rose from the long covered porch and came toward us barking and wagging his tail in an excess of nervous energy.

"Buck," Stephen warned the dog.

"Hullo, Buck," I said, putting my hand out. I was prepared for rejection here too; Buck was pretty much a one-man's dog. But he snuffled my hand with his cold snout, and made that funny growling that Chessies do when they're pleased to see you. "He remembers me," I said, foolishly pleased.

"Yes," Stephen said. "He never was much use as a guard dog."

I laughed, and then Stephen smiled too—wryly. Buck nuzzled my fingers, pushed past and thrust his nose in my crotch, and I jumped—which hurt the ribs and the leg…considerably.

"Goddamn it, Buck," Stephen said, shoving the dog away, still keeping hold of me.

There were several funny things I could have said but I just stood there stupidly, and something changed in Stephen's hold. Grew…kind.

"You *are* tired," he said from a distance.

"Yes," I agreed politely. My eyes kept closing although I wanted to look at him, explain—or just show him I was paying attention.

Very important that last bit. Very important.

"Mark?" Stephen said from the other end of the tunnel.

The next time I opened my eyes I was lying on an examining table in a doctor's office. Like one of those kinky dreams. Stephen leaned over me. I couldn't see his expression—there was a bright light blazing over his shoulder—but he was holding my cock. I smiled at him, encouraging him to do something besides hold me in that cool, clinical grip. Just that was making me hard though.

And then I realized that he was furious. Not just furious. There was something like fear in his shadowy face.

"What's wrong?" I asked, trying to sit up. I realized that I was naked—that I had no idea where my pistol was. That was like a totally different kind of dream.

I shoved Stephen's restraining hand aside, the tissue rustling loudly as I rolled off the table—and then crumpled to the cold tile floor as my leg gave way. The pain nearly blacked me out again; I balanced there on my hands and knees, taking deep breaths.

"What the hell is *wrong* with you?" Stephen said. He sounded almost distraught.

Bewildered, I raised my head to stare up at him. I gasped, "I thought something was wrong."

He was looking at me as though I'd shinnied down the bed sheets when the orderlies weren't watching.

"I thought you were in trouble," I said. The surge of adrenaline drained away, leaving me sick and shivering. My heart was racing in fight-or-flight response. Could you have a heart attack at twenty-nine? Could you keel over from plain old exhaustion?

Incredulously, he said, "You thought *I*…?" Whatever he saw in my face must have convinced him I was speaking the simple truth. "Sweet Jesus," he muttered, bending over me. "Lovers and madmen." He half-lifted me up. I'd forgotten how strong he was. It was startling. I resisted the desire to wrap my arms around his neck and refuse to let him go, cooperating instead in getting to my feet and clambering onto the table again.

Stephen helped me lower myself to the crumpled tissue covering the padding. My ribs protested forcibly. An assortment of hitherto unacknowledged aches and pains announced their arrival, and I swore. Loudly.

Stephen swore right back. “Goddamn it, Mark. What the hell’s the matter with you?”

It had a rhetorical ring to it. I said, “You’re the doctor. You tell me.”

“Well, let’s start with the physical,” he said. “At least we can fix that. You’ve got a bruise on your right cheekbone where someone punched you. You’ve got two cracked ribs where you were kicked. I can tell that from the boot-shaped bruises on your chest and back and hip. Assorted lacerations, scrapes, contusions. And a stab wound in your inner thigh—from a screwdriver, according to you—where someone tried to carve your dick off. There’s a scrape…” He stroked a gentle finger along the length of my cock—which twitched wearily in response. “You look like a piece of carved meat.”

I wished he’d keep brushing my cock with that delicate tracing touch. I wished he’d wrap those long, cool fingers around me and work me with that easy expertise I remembered so well—or, better yet, take me into his mouth. I used to dream about that minty-fresh mouth of his and the things it did to me.

“Garden parties,” I said. “They do take it out of a bloke.”

He shook his head, not seeing the humor. Which was sad because before we’d always managed to find something to laugh about.

All at once I felt very tired. Old. I closed my eyes, closed out the harsh lights and Stephen’s grim face. If I lay very still, I’d be okay. It was only moving that hurt. And thinking. And breathing. And as much as this hurt, it was better than the alternative. That was the rumor anyway.

"Can you manage to walk upstairs?"

I opened my eyes and caught his expression before it changed. And I thought then that perhaps the rumors were greatly exaggerated, because Stephen looked sorry for me, and I wasn't sure I could take that.

"Of course," I said. I wondered what he'd do if I said I couldn't manage it. Would he carry me? Sweep me up the stairs like Rhett Butler scooping up Scarlett O'Hara? The idea held a certain charm. He must have lugged me in from the front yard—and what a pity I'd missed it. Better not to try my luck or his patience again. He was liable to leave me here in the cold.

He moved away, returned with a little paper cup full of water. "Here. I know you don't like pain pills, but take these."

I sat up, peeled the tissue paper off my damp skin. I took the offered cup, popped the pills, and washed them down with lukewarm water.

He was saying briskly, "I've stitched up your thigh again, given you a tetanus booster and a vitamin B shot and pumped you full of antibiotics. I should retape your ribs."

"Nah. They feel wonderful," I assured him. I was wondering how long I'd been out. More than a minute or two, clearly. I touched the dressing on my thigh. "Did you stitch a secret message into the embroidery?"

His mouth twitched, but it wasn't really a smile. I moved gingerly off the examining table, and he steadied me. I couldn't help myself. I reached for him. Slung an arm around his shoulder and leaned into him, pressing my face in the curve of his neck—just holding him.

Stephen didn't move, neither rejecting nor accepting, just standing still, breathing quietly, steadily. His skin was warm and smooth against my face, and I could feel the pulse in his throat and hear his even exhalations. I could smell his aftershave, and that faint persistent hint of antiseptic and mouthwash, and the cottony-laundered scent of his polo shirt.

After a time he put his arm around me and stroked my back, the weight of his hand slow and soothing down the length of my spine. He didn't say anything, and neither did I; we just stood there.

Finally I pulled away. I could feel him searching my face, and I was glad that there was nothing to see.

"You just need a good night's sleep," he said.

I didn't remember the guestroom, although I don't suppose it had changed since J.E.B. Stuart last slept there. It was a large, sunny, second-floor suite with a view of the old magnolia trees and the little lake beyond. There was a lot of spindly cherrywood furniture and white wallpaper with tiny violets.

Stephen helped me into the bed, and I inched myself around trying to get comfortable. The feather mattress was like sinking into a cloud, and I couldn't help groaning my relief. I closed my eyes. *Heaven.*

"Yell if you need anything," he said.

I smiled, not bothering to open my eyes.

I thought he'd gone away but then he put his hand on my forehead. It felt nice. Cool. He brushed the back of his hand against my cheek. Pleasant to be on the receiving end of this attention, so I didn't bother to assure him that I was perfectly all right.

Perhaps he thought I was already asleep. He ran his hand lightly over my hair. A slow caressing sweep. And then again. I kept my eyes closed. I figured if I opened them he'd stop, and the feel of his cool dry hand stroking my skin and hair was wonderful. I thought of a line from *Little Dorrit*: "It came like magic in a pint bottle; it was not ecstasy but it was comfort."

I didn't make the mistake of making too much of this comfort. I recognized the impersonal kindness of it—like a vet might stroke a tranquilized tiger. But I kept still and soaked it up and the next thing I knew I was waking from what felt like a long, deep sleep.

The dying afternoon sun streamed through the window, bathing the room in the last rays of golden light. I turned my head on the feather pillow, feeling crisp linen beneath my scraped cheek, my battered body cushioned and comforted by the down duvet and the plump mattress. It was like being in a cocoon. It felt…safe.

For quite a while I lay there not thinking at all, simply enjoying that feeling of well-being, listening to the peaceful sounds of the coming evening in an elegant old house.

A long way from the fiery winds and dust storms of arid Kandahar. But I didn't want to think about Afghanistan now. Didn't want to think about Barry Shelton. Didn't want to think about cities in rubble or crying women—Afghan women, English women—didn't want to think about fields of bloodred poppies, or hand-held heat-seeking missiles, or ancient statues blasted into oblivion.

The world will not find rest by simply saying "Peace." Just like the bastard to quote an Afghan proverb at me. But I didn't want to think of the Old Man. Couldn't. I turned my head, relaxing as I spotted my Glock lying within easy reach on the nightstand. The magazine was beside it, and I smiled faintly despite the clear message of Stephen's disapproval.

I used to think about Stephen nearly every night before I fell asleep. I liked picturing him in this old, comfortable house in this quiet corner of the world. It was comforting somehow to think of him here, to think of how far removed he was, how safe he was, from everything I knew. From everything I was.

It had kept me centered, focused, believing that I could one day come back here and be part of this life—of Stephen's life. In a way it had given me the strength to keep doing what I had to do.

The lacy curtains across the windows stirred gently in the breeze. It was cool now. The humid heat of the day was only a fever memory. Outside the window, birds twittered in the trees, settling down for the night. Homely sounds floated up from the kitchen. The beams and rafters popped like cracking knuckles. The scent of magnolias drifted through the open window—and suddenly I was restless.

I tossed off the duvet, sat up wincing, favoring the ribs. The sight of my bruised, bandaged body in the oval mirror over the dresser was startling. I eased out of the bed and padded over to the mirror.

I spy with my little eye…

Something starting with "B." Broken? Bruises? Blood?

I looked like I'd been beaten within an inch of my life—which was not far from the truth. It was only seeing it through Stephen's eyes that made me realize…

And I was a lot luckier than Barry Shelton. Or Arsullah Hakim. But I wasn't going to think about Barry. Or Mrs. Shelton throwing a peeler—and then the bowl of potato peelings—at me. I was out of it. I was safe. I was home.

Except…as Stephen pointed out, this wasn't my home.

I examined a foot-shaped bruise over my hip and then looked up into my mirrored eyes. My expression gave me pause. I looked…different…but I couldn't define how. I looked tired, of course. Black shadows under my eyes—and the beard looked alien now. The bruise on my cheekbone didn't help, but *British GQ* wouldn't have been pounding on my door in any case. I didn't remotely resemble Pierce Brosnan or Daniel Craig. Nor did I want to. In my line of work, the less memorable the better. Looking like everyone else was an advantage, and in Afghanistan dark-haired, dark-eyed, sharp-featured, slightly-built men of medium height were very much everyone else.

Turning from the mirror, I hunted for something to wear. My bag sat by the dresser, but the blood-soaked jeans were nowhere to be found. Nor were the clothes I had been wearing when I arrived. Probably down in Stephen's examining room. I found a robe hanging in the antique wardrobe and pulled it on. It was too big for me, but I liked it. It smelled faintly of Stephen's soap, although I suppose that was really the scent of his laundry detergent.

Making my way downstairs, I found Stephen in the kitchen. He was grilling steaks with onions and tomatoes—British style, the way I liked them—and my heart lifted a little.

"Smells good," I said.

He glanced around quickly. "I didn't hear you."

No one ever heard me. That was the point. I said, "That's the best sleep I've had in a long time."

"It's the *only* sleep you've had in a long time," he said dryly. "I thought you'd be out for another hour at least. I was going to bring you something on a tray."

"Not necessary." I limped over to the table and sat down. I hadn't realized how hungry I was until I smelled food cooking. I tried to remember the last time I'd eaten. It was a little vague. Someone had given me an ORP on the military transport plane, and the Old Man had offered me tea during my debriefing. Tea. That seemed comical. Scones and sandwiches and tea. I'd thrown them all up in the toilet on my way out of the building.

It occurred to me that by now everyone would be well aware I hadn't turned myself in for medical evaluation and treatment. But of course they'd have already known. They'd have known about my visit to Devon and Barry Shelton's mother within the hour.

I said, talking myself away from it, "I wasn't sure you'd be here. I thought you might have been called into the hospital."

"It's just a little community hospital," he said. "Twenty-five beds."

"You're not at Winchester Medical Center now?"

"No." His eyes were very green and very direct. "I decided it was time to make a few changes in my life."

"Ah." That would have been the last birthday. The milestone birthday where he turned fifty. I offered a smile, but he had turned back to the stove.

Stephen continued to prepare our supper; he could have been by himself for all the attention he paid me, and yet it was rather relaxing. I liked watching him. He was built well. Strong but not burly. He moved with a sort of easy, long-limbed grace. Comfortable in his skin. I liked his quiet and his calm. The mark of maturity, I thought. He had worked out what he wanted from life and he was at ease with his choices, with who he was. But then he had fought for that privilege. His family had wanted very different things for him.

The longing to put my arms around him, hold him was like a physical hunger. Worse than physical hunger, actually. I warned myself to be patient, to give him time. I said, "I appreciate your letting me stay, Stephen."

"You didn't leave me much choice."

I stared at the wooden tabletop, looking for answers in generations-worth of crackling veneer. "No. I suppose not. There aren't many people I can trust."

"Oh, it's about trust?" His tone was unpromising.

"It is rather."

Silence. Stephen turned the stove off, dished out food, set a plate in front of me, and sat down on the other side of the table. He speared a bite of steak, chewed ferociously, swallowed, and then said very quietly, "You've got a fucking nerve talking to me about trust."

As my own mouth was full, I had to chew fast, swallow—and he interrupted before I could speak.

"I don't know what happened to you. I'm sure you have no intention of telling me. But it's obvious you need a little breathing space. So I'll give you that. I'll give you time to rest and recover from whatever the hell is the latest disaster. But when you're back on your feet, I want you gone, Mark. You understand? You can stay here till then, but after that you're on your own."

I stared at his face, unfamiliar in its hardness. I had done that. I had I made him hard and bitter. But surely he realized I hadn't meant to. Hadn't meant to hurt him, to let him down, to betray the thing between us because I knew—yes, even *I* knew—how rare that thing between us was.

I said, "Don't I get to —"

"*No,* you don't." His eyes met mine with anger as black as the inside of an oil barrel.

"Right." It occurred to me that he was the only person on the planet I was afraid of. And he was the gentlest man I'd ever known.

Don't push him, I thought. *Don't crowd him.* I picked up my fork and made myself continue eating.

For a time there was nothing but the scrape of silverware on china, the creak of chairs and the heavy old table.

I put my fork down. "Look, Stephen. You're not —"

"Two fucking years, Mark." He was coming right back at me without skipping a step; and even I could hardly miss that this was a fury that had been building for months. "And I don't want to hear anything about having a chance to tell your side of it. I gave you every possible opportunity. You know what the last thing you said to me was? You said you couldn't talk."

The unfairness of that left me feeling winded, and for a flash I was back brawling in the sand with someone's boot in my guts. I barely remembered the phone conversation Stephen referred to. It had taken place four months ago. Right before I left for Afghanistan. I'd been distracted, preoccupied—naturally.

I said, "I was preparing for an OPO, for God's sake!"

He stared at me like I was mad. "You still don't get it, Mark. That wasn't the *opening* dialog, that was the closing. The end. That was your last chance."

"I don't —"

"Understand? I know. You really don't. The truth is there were two years before that last operation—or whatever OPO means—and you couldn't find time to talk then either. Two years. Two *years*."

Two years?

Had it really been two years? Yes, I suppose it must have been. And I suppose that did explain some of Stephen's anger.

He waited for me to say something. All at once I was very tired. Too tired to think of a good answer. Probably because there wasn't a good answer. And a bad answer might mean the loss of any last chance to save this thing. I picked up my fork and made myself continue eating.

The steak was cooked exactly the way I liked. It was good. My brain assured me of that. My mouth told me it was pencil shavings.

I could feel Stephen staring at me, could feel his disbelieving silence. But when I said nothing he gave a short, disbelieving laugh and also resumed eating.

We finished our meal without further conversation.

"Can I help with the dishes?" I asked, as he cleared my plate away.

He put the dishes in the sink and said brusquely, "Lena Roosevelt comes in tomorrow morning. She'll take care of it."

He glanced at me, and I knew he was waiting to see whether I remembered who Lena Roosevelt was.

"I remember Lena," I said. And I did. Sort of. She was a large, motherly black woman who had worked for Stephen's family since Stephen had been at school.

"Good. Because I'll be at the hospital all day tomorrow, and I don't want you pulling a gun on her and scaring her out of her wits."

"I rarely shoot the domestic staff," I assured him. "I know good help is hard to find." Truthfully, I thought it would take a lot more than a man with a gun to scare the wits out of Lena Roosevelt.

He turned back to the sink without comment. I stared at the long, unapproachable line of his back. Sometimes words merely complicated what was really quite a simple issue. I took a step forward and he said, "If you put your arms around me, I'll knock you down, so help me God."

I stopped.

Words then. I just needed to find the right words.

The sprinklers came on outside, filling the silence. And still Stephen didn't face me.

I was supposed to be a pretty good negotiator, and yet I couldn't think of any argument that would reach him in this mood. I was too tired. That was the trouble. Once I'd caught up on my sleep I'd see the situation more clearly, find the right way to approach him.

He couldn't have changed in his feelings for me that fast.

Two years.

"I think I'll lie down for a bit," I said.

Stephen's hair was soft as silk, like spun silver threading through my fingers. I needed to touch, needed that connection because the pleasure of that mouth sucking strongly on my cock was almost frightening in its intensity. Hot wet delight of mouth on the pulsing heartbeat of my prick. Nothing should feel that good…sheer sensation sending me spinning out of control—overwhelming to feel this much. Dangerous. I gazed down into Stephen's smiling eyes. All the warmth, all the love, all the tenderness —

"Mark."

I opened my eyes at once. It was nearly dark, the twilight shadows lengthening into night. I was lying on a bed in a strange room. My pistol was…to the right of me within hand's reach. But I didn't move toward it; the voice in my dream had been Stephen's.

And then I realized that it was not a dream. At least…disappointment vibrated through my neurons like the tongue of a mournful bell…I was not alone in the room. A pale blur stood in the doorway of the bedroom—and I remembered everything that had happened in the past four days.

Unbelievably—against all odds—I was really here. In Stephen's home.

"Yes?" I moved to sit—and then put my hand to my side as my cracked ribs reminded me of recent events.

Stephen said, "Don't get up. I just wanted to make sure you don't need anything before I leave."

"Before you leave?" I repeated, trying to make sense of that.

"I'm going out for a few hours. I have plans for the evening."

"Plans?"

Simple English but I couldn't seem to translate. A note in his voice sent a warning prickle down my spine. There was no reason he shouldn't have plans. Stephen had a lot of friends—and a lot of responsibilities.

"Yes," he said in that elaborately casual tone. "I'll be back after midnight, and I'll probably be gone before you're awake in the morning, but I'll ring you tomorrow around lunch time."

"All right." But my sense of unease grew.

He turned to leave—then turned back. "Are you sure you're all right by yourself tonight?"

What on earth…?

I said gravely, "One night of my own company won't drive me to put a bullet in my brain."

"Not funny," he said.

Wasn't it? Probably not. I said, "I'm fine. I expect I'll sleep right through."

I could feel his hesitation. It was a little annoying, actually. Didn't he believe me? Did he not trust me with the mint julep glasses? What was the problem?

"I'll see you tomorrow," he said finally.

I murmured something, waiting until he had returned downstairs, waiting until I heard the front door close. Getting out of bed, ignoring my body's protest, I limped across the hall to the bedroom that looked down over the drive.

The porch light gleamed off the sterling of Stephen's hair as he walked down the steps. There was another man with him. They were talking in low voices, but I heard Stephen's husky laugh.

They crossed the drive to the sports car parked there. The second man, shorter and heavier than Stephen, unlocked the passenger side door, turning away. Stephen reached for him, and they kissed briefly.

The pain felt removed, almost distant. A little worse than the leg, a little less than the ribs. Bearable if I didn't think about it or move suddenly.

Stephen lowered himself into car. The other man crossed around to the driver's side. The car engine came on, the headlights illuminated a stone statue on the lawn. Pulling way quietly, the car disappeared down the drive.

I watched the red taillights till they disappeared from sight.

Two years was a long time. A very long time.

Chapter Three

The sound of a vacuum cleaner moving through the downstairs rooms…I opened my eyes to bright sunlight and the sound of birds outside the window. It was already warm but it was the gentle warmth of late spring in a civilized country—and for a few seconds I couldn't think where the hell I was—like one of those novels where the hero wakes up on a different planet or fifty years in the past. I blinked up at the old-fashioned ceiling fan whispering overhead.

Then it all came rushing back. We'd been rolled up. The operation had gone bad, Barry and I had been arrested. It played out in my memory like a film: the ambush, our capture, our escape—Barry's death.

I tried to put the pieces in order. The last four days seemed like a dream. A fever-dream. But two points were very clear: I had made straight for Stephen like a homing pigeon—and I was essentially AWOL. I had done a runner. I was playing E&E with my own team. I lay still absorbing it, dealing with it.

It took some absorbing.

Downstairs the vacuum turned off. I heard the back screen door bang open and shut, and then the dull thud of what sounded like someone beating a rug.

Shoving off the bedclothes, I hobbled over to the window and looked down on the yard below. I could see the top of Lena Roosevelt's gray head. She was whaling away with a broom on one of Stephen's antique Persian rugs. Buck pelted around her in a giant circle, apparently unable to contain his excitement. Divots of grass flew up beneath his feet as he rocketed around the yard. Lena directed an occasional acerbic comment his way.

For a time I watched her, watched the dog slow and eventually lose interest. He trotted down to the lake to harass the geese. It was peaceful. The sunlight flickering on the leaves of the hickory and magnolias had a soporific effect. But I'd slept plenty in the last twenty-four hours. It was time to pull myself together. Especially since my defection was unlikely to go unremarked. Interestingly, I cared less about what the Old Man would have to say than the fact that Stephen had promised to ring around lunch time. The brass alarm clock on the dresser indicated it was nearly eleven o'clock.

I shrugged into the navy bathrobe and made my way down the hallway. The door to Stephen's room was closed. I hesitated, but continued on. I could find out what I needed to know without resorting to that. And if I couldn't...well, there was always that.

In the guest bathroom was a big, old-fashioned claw-foot bathtub and a bottle of tropical bubble bath on the windowsill. The "rain-flower scented" bubble bath—which didn't seem at all Stephen's kind of thing—proclaimed the merits of kukui nut oil and vitamin E. I poured a generous amount into a couple of inches of hot water and carefully lowered myself in.

I couldn't afford to get my stitches or the taping around my ribs wet, but no way was I going to settle for soap and flannel. Whatever rain-flower scent was, it had to be an improvement over sweat and blood and whatever else I stank of. I splashed around in the few inches of water, scrubbed up the best I could, then hauled myself out. It took a while to shave off the beard. When at last it was gone and I'd rinsed the last whiskery traces down the sink, I stared at myself. The pallor of my jaw and chin was in marked contrast to the rest of my face. But there was something else. I looked closer. What was it? Why did that man in the mirror not look like…me?

Uneasily, I re-donned the bathrobe, heading downstairs.

I found Lena in the kitchen doing dishes. I knocked on the door frame in an effort not to startle her. She glanced over her shoulder and there was no particular pleasure in her face.

"Morning, Mr. Hardwicke. Dr. Thorpe said you were visiting."

She was a tall, big-boned black woman of about seventy. She had handsome, rather severe features—definitely severe at the moment—and iron gray hair in a tight bun. She wore wire spectacles, sensible shoes, and a cotton dress with blue flowers. She didn't appear to have aged a day in two years. I, on the other hand, felt a lifetime had passed.

"Lovely to see you again too, Mrs. Roosevelt," I said, gently mocking that disapproving tone. "How's the family?"

Her mouth tightened. "My family is fine, Mr. Hardwicke. Dr. Thorpe said to make you a good breakfast when you woke up. What would you like?"

A time machine? Failing that, I'd have liked Lena as an ally, but that obviously wasn't going to happen. I said, "Anything is fine. You haven't seen my clothes by any chance?"

"Your jeans are in the dryer now. I believe I got all the bloodstains out." Her mouth compressed in further censure. "Dr. Thorpe left a shirt for you." She nodded to where a white shirt on a wire hanger hung on one of the kitchen cupboard doors. "I can fix you eggs, French toast, pancakes…"

"Anything, really. Tea would be nice, but I can —"

No, I couldn't. Her look stopped me cold. I was not a member of this family. I was a guest. An unwelcome guest at that.

I took the shirt, got my jeans from the dryer, and went upstairs to change. When I came back downstairs bacon was frying in a pan and Lena was dipping bread in a bowl. The kitchen was redolent with cinnamon and nutmeg and bacon. Pulling out a chair at the table, I said, "That smells good. I guess I'm hungrier than I thought."

She sniffed, unmollified.

I gave her just enough time to forget about me sitting quietly at the table. She turned the bacon, put the egg-soaked bread in another pan, turned the heat down on the whistling tea kettle.

"How is Stephen? Is he all right?" I asked neutrally.

There was a little pause. She said without looking at me, "Dr. Thorpe is just fine."

"Does he like working at the new hospital?"

Her profile softened minutely as she poured tea into a white china cup. “Yes, he does.”

I watched without comment as she splashed milk in my tea and sugared it appropriately. How the hell could she have possibly remembered how I took my tea?

She brought the cup to me. I asked, “Is he still on the Save the Battlefields Committee?”

“He’s a member of the Battlefields Foundation, yes.” Her mouth twitched a little. I’d always suspected that, like me, she appreciated the wry humor in that.

“And the Arts Council? And the Theater Guild?”

I was teasing, but she wasn’t having any of the bonhomie stuff. “The Thorpes have lived in this valley for a long time. Mr. Stephen—Dr. Thorpe—is an important man to this community.”

“Yes.” I said, “He’s important to me too.”

She gave me a look then, but said nothing, turning back to the stove and flipping the toasting bread.

“I take it he’s seeing someone now?”

I knew it was a difficult question. Stephen’s sexual orientation had been a problem for his politically-connected family, and while Stephen didn’t hide it, he didn’t flaunt it. Lena had been very kind to me when I was with Stephen, which led me to believe her sympathies had always been with him, but now I was an outsider, and talking about such a sensitive topic presented a quandary for her.

I didn’t think she was going to answer, but finally she said curtly, “Yes.”

"Do you like him?"

That offended her sensibilities on so many levels she didn't know where to start. She finally spluttered, "Mr. Boxer is a very nice young gentleman. I *do* like him, not that my likes or dislikes amount to a hill of beans."

By which I gathered that if Lena'd had her druthers, I wouldn't be staying at Thorpe House. I didn't care about that. What interested me was that Mr. Boxer was not a doctor, and he was "young," which I took to mean younger than Stephen. But was he younger than me? Because Stephen had fretted a bit about the age difference between us.

I watched her flip the French toast onto a plate and sprinkle it with powdered sugar and cinnamon. She piled on the bacon and carried the plate to the table, positioning it perfectly on the lace placemat in front of me.

"I'm glad," I said. "Stephen's happiness matters to me."

And it did, but she was right to give me that that grim look over the top of her glasses.

"Stephen Bodean Thorpe." He was grinning.

"But that's nothing," I scoffed. "Try going through life with a last name like Hardwicke."

He laughed, and I leaned forward and kissed him hard. I loved the way he tasted, a little different from everyone else. Clean and cool with a hint of spearmint. He kissed me hard back, insinuating his tongue into my mouth, and I shuddered in his arms.

He laughed again—and I could taste that too—and withdrew. "That bad?"

"That good." And I covered his mouth once more.

The screen door banged and I was suddenly sitting on the back porch swing, throwing a tennis ball to Buck, and avoiding thinking about all the things I should have been thinking about.

"Doctor Thorpe calling for you," Lena said crisply. She brought the phone to me and I pushed the button. I took a deep breath, let it out. "Hullo," I said. "I believe I owe you an apology."

After a beat, Stephen said, "How are you feeling?"

I was astonished at the way my heart had sped up at the sound of his voice. A Pavlovian response if there ever was one. "Much better, thanks. Listen, Stephen, I'm sorry about yesterday. Sorry for forcing my company on you. I…haven't…been myself for a few days."

I read wariness and surprise in his silence. He said finally, "No, I realized that. You made it clear enough four months ago that this was the last place you wanted—or intended to be." He didn't sound angry…just stating a fact.

I said, "Maybe my subconscious knew something I didn't."

That time he barely paused, saying briskly, "I'll be home for supper, but I'll be out again this evening. Anything you'd like me to bring you? I can rent a movie or something."

I said over my disappointment, "Thanks, yes. A film would be terrific. Nothing with guns. Nothing set in the Middle East. Something from Merchant and Ivory, perhaps. I've got some catching up to do."

That was a little obvious on my part. We'd watched *Maurice* together the first night I had come to dinner here—started to watch it, anyway. We never did get through the film. The evening had ended upstairs in Stephen's bedroom. We'd fucked, slept, woke around midnight and ate the pecan pie and ice cream that we hadn't had for dessert. Then we'd fucked again—only by then we'd been making love.

"Got it," Stephen said. "Some kind of costume drama about a handsome Englishman fucking up his life and everyone else's. I'll see what I can find."

It was my turn to pause. Into my silence, he said —crisp and businesslike, "Stay off the leg as much as possible. I'll see you tonight."

He rang off.

Lena insisted on fixing me lunch, although I'd only had breakfast a few hours earlier. I ate enough to avoid insulting her, and then realized I was dead tired again. My body craved sleep like a drug. I'd never experienced anything like it.

Hauling myself upstairs, I stretched out on the four-poster bed. I wondered how long it would take for our lads to track me down. Not long. The Old Man probably already knew where I was. I wondered what he would do—and why I wasn't more worried about it. I was still wondering when I drifted off.

"You're not seriously worried about the age difference?"

"I could be your father."

"I like older men. I like the fact that you're experienced." I kissed the bridge of his nose. "I like the fact that you're wise."

He snorted. "If I was wise I wouldn't —"

I didn't want to hear that. I cut him off, covering his lips with mine, distracting him and losing myself for a few seconds in that sweet mingling of breath and lips. "And bloody sexy," I added.

He was smiling, but ruefully. "Then again you've got a thing for older men, don't you?"

"Only you. I'm saving my thing for you." I nipped his lower lip, and he sucked in a sharp breath. "Want to see my thing, Stephen?"

It was after five when I woke again. The shadows in the room had lengthened, and I could smell something mouth-watering cooking downstairs. I realized that Stephen must be home, and I felt that mix of anticipation and anxiety as I rose and made my halting way downstairs.

He was in the kitchen pouring a glass of wine. He looked handsome and successful—and absolutely untouchable—in charcoal trousers and a pale blue shirt with sleeves pushed up to bare his tanned, muscular arms.

He glanced up as the floorboard squeaked, instantly on guard. But his voice was pleasant enough. "Well, you look about a hundred percent better."

"I feel about a hundred percent better." I took a chair at the table under his critical eye. A DVD lay next to the bowl of fruit: *The Fellowship of the Ring.*

"How's the leg?" he asked.

"Mending. The ribs hurt more, tell you the truth." I picked up the DVD. "*Lord of the Rings*?"

"Have you seen it?" He sipped his wine, observing me with those elven-green eyes.

"No."

"You'll enjoy it. There's a lot of dragon slaying."

"Sounds like my kind of thing."

"That was my thought."

"May I have a glass of wine?"

"You shouldn't." He went ahead and poured a glass for me. I sipped it while he returned to the stove.

"Dinner is just about ready," he said. "Beef stroganoff."

I wasn't hungry. I hadn't been hungry in months, although he was a very good cook—off-hand I couldn't think of anything he didn't do well. "I could have fixed myself something," I told him. "Since you've got plans."

He didn't respond.

"So do I get to meet him?"

"Who?" He was frowning.

I said lightly, "The new man in your life."

"Conducting a surveillance op on me now?"

I said, "Believe it or not —"

"I don't believe it," he cut across. "So let's not go there."

"I'm…trying to be civil." It was harder than it should have been to dredge up a smile. For someone who made a living dissembling I was having a hell of a time.

"I don't need you to be civil. I just need you to tell me exactly what your plans are."

It was a simple enough question but it felt as though someone had unplugged me from the mains. I could feel the life and energy draining away. Some of it must have shown in my face, because his brows drew together. When he spoke again, his tone was quite different. "Mark, what the hell has happened? It's obvious something has."

I shook my head. "It's nothing. I'm…burnt out, is all. Need a holiday. A rest cure." I smiled. "I already feel loads better. You noticed yourself."

To my surprise, he pulled out a chair and sat down cattycorner from me—close enough that our knees brushed. "You said you were in trouble on the phone. What kind of trouble?"

It wasn't fair. He was close enough to pull into my arms. I could see the reluctant concern on his face, the kindness there—despite his desire and intention to remain detached. And I was desperate enough to take kindness tonight—if it came from Stephen. I was acutely aware of the way his hair curled over the back of his collar, of the broad muscular shoulders and smooth chest beneath the tailored shirt, of the scent of faded aftershave and mint which on him was peculiarly erotic.

I swallowed down my yearning, my loneliness—and surprised myself by telling the truth. "I'm…not ready to talk about it yet. Can't. Not even to you. Is that all right?"

His face changed, and fleetingly there was something there that made my own heart light with hope. "Of course it's all right."

"Thank you." And there was no doubt I meant it. Embarrassing.

He nodded, squeezed the knee of my good leg, and rose.

The meal was good. Noodles and beef made a pleasant change from lamb and chicken and rice—you eat a lot of rice in Afghanistan. Rice and stews. Qormas, they call them. I did my best to eat because I knew Stephen was observing me with that professional eye. Inexplicably, telling him I couldn't talk to him was finally the right move because he was much more relaxed, almost friendly. He talked about his work at the hospital, and about his day. It was all very ordinary and normal, and it gave me a chance to pull myself together. I was realistic enough to know that that was probably why he was doing it, that he was now viewing me in a professional light, putting aside his personal antipathy for the time being.

And I played to that quite shamelessly. I let him win tired smiles from me, let him distract me from my preoccupied silences, made myself swallow food I didn't want when he glanced at my plate. Except…it wasn't really playing. The guile here was in deliberately lowering my guard to let him see…the truth. That I was worried and afraid. And I was…except that I couldn't feel it. But I knew how to act it, and so I did—for Stephen's benefit.

It seemed to work. After the meal he showed me how to operate the new VCR/DVD player in the den, got me settled on the wide sofa with extra pillows and a throw rug, and told me where to find the microwave popcorn or the ice cream should I be so inclined.

He wasn't warm, but he was more than the grudging host he'd been. It was nice for a change, although I couldn't help remembering the nights we'd cuddled on this same sofa watching films and talking about nothing. Nothing more important than what we were going to do with the rest of our lives. At that time it had seemed a joint decision.

I wondered what would have happened if I hadn't left. If I hadn't let the Old Man talk me into one last job. That was rather funny to think of two years later. One last job which had somehow turned into…eleven assignments. So in the end, Stephen had been right. I wonder if he got any satisfaction out of it. Maybe he'd convinced himself it was all for the best. Maybe he told himself there was no proof we'd have stayed together even if I hadn't left.

Having got me settled to his satisfaction, Stephen went upstairs to change, and I turned on the film I had no desire to see, and let my thoughts roam. They didn't roam far. They seemed knobbled these days.

"I'd pretty much given up on you ever showing up."

I shivered. He pulled me close, chuckling. I liked the fact that he was physically demonstrative, open about his feelings—just the opposite of me. Just the opposite of nearly every man I knew. I rested my head on his shoulder, lulled by the tenderness he offered so easily.

He murmured against my ear, "Of course it hadn't occurred to me that you were still growing up."

I sat up, punched his shoulder. "Leave off, Stephen. I'm not a bleeding toddler!"

And he'd laughed. We'd laughed a lot. More than I could remember laughing with anyone.

Stephen came back downstairs, but didn't come into the den. I heard him moving around in the kitchen, heard him go out the front. I wondered if he was slipping out without saying goodnight, but a few minutes later he was back—and he had company.

"Mark, this is Bryce," he introduced. "Bryce Boxer, Mark Hardwicke."

Bryce. Christ.

I got up fast from the sofa—ignoring the wrench of ribs and leg—and startling them both. Even before I saw Stephen's expression or heard Bryce's, "Oh hey, we shouldn't have disturbed you, Mark!" I had myself back under control.

"A pleasure to meet you," I said, offering my hand.

Bryce was nice-looking. Attractive, not handsome. Thinning blond hair, blue eyes, about my height but stocky, midforties. He looked successful, assured, and happy. You don't see a lot of happy in my business.

Easy target, I summed him up.

His handshake was firm, his fingers and palm uncallused. So he didn't do a lot of driving or any manual labor. Stockbroker, teacher, architect—I could see him in any of those positions. I could see him face down in the dirt, too, with a hole blown through his back.

"Nice to meet you too," he said. "I've heard a lot about you."

What the fuck did that mean?

"You have the advantage of me," I said ruefully, and he laughed with me. Stephen did not laugh. Stephen watched me closely.

"So you're English," Bryce observed. "I love your accent. My college roommate was English." I waited for him to ask me if I knew a bloke named X, but he refrained. "Stevie said you had some kind of accident." There was curiosity in his eyes.

I cooled down a fraction. It was all right—that part of it anyway—Stephen wasn't going to say anything to compromise me. He'd grown up in Washington. He might not approve of what I did for a living, but he wasn't going to burn me. And of course he'd have had to say something to explain my presence.

"Yes," I said. And unobligingly left it at that.

Bryce's brows rose, but he was smiling. "It's a shame you're not getting to see any of the sights."

Stephen had told him about me, and Bryce was relaxed, friendly, and unthreatened. He was confident of Stephen. Confident they had something I couldn't touch. It worried me like nothing else had.

"I've seen the best ones," I replied, and I smiled at Stephen.

"We should be going if we don't want to miss the start," Stephen said.

Bryce glanced at his watch. "You're right." To me he explained, "We're seeing the Smithsonian Jazz Masterworks Ensemble."

"Oh, jolly good!" I said.

"Okay, let's go," Stephen said, reading me correctly.

Bryce shrugged, untroubled at being hustled away. "Nice to have met you, Mark. Take care now."

"Always," I said.

Stephen was back a few moments later.

"He seems nice enough," I said, having resettled myself carefully on the sofa. "Does he know you hate jazz?"

He ignored that. "I'll see you tomorrow evening."

"Not planning on coming home?"

"If you've got any sense at all you'll be asleep before then."

"Oh, but I'll want to hear all about the Smithsonian Jazz Masterworks Ensemble."

He said flatly, "I knew this was a mistake. But Bryce wanted to meet you."

That brought me up short. "Of course. Why shouldn't we meet? Come on, Stephen, I'd like to think we were friends—at the very least."

He looked unconvinced.

"How long have you been seeing each other?" I asked.

It was a perfectly reasonable question, and I asked in a perfectly friendly tone of voice, but apparently Stephen knew me pretty well.

"Mark." I could see him thinking of how he wanted to say it: how to make his point without destroying the fragile truce between us. "Let's get something clear. You don't…have any rights here. I let you come because you begged, because you're in some kind of trouble. For old time's sake, that's all."

I smiled. "How long?"

Irritably, he answered, "Seven weeks."

Seven weeks. Not long. Not…established. And practically on the rebound. Still vulnerable to attack whatever Brent—Bryce, whatever it was—though.

I smiled again—and, reading that smile, Stephen said, "Don't think it, Mark. You're the one who'll be hurt this time."

Chapter Four

Machine gun fire ripped through the night, I could hear it hitting the Jeep. Arsullah Hakim's face was illuminated in the headlamps, his blackened teeth, the scar through his eyebrow, flecks of spit in his beard as he cursed me. My fingers slipped in the blood from his broken nose as I tried to gouge his eye out. Dimly, I was aware of Arabic voices crying out and Shelton yelling, of the rocks jabbing into my back as the Taliban and I rolled around in the dirt, grappling for the screwdriver. The driver lay dead a few feet from us—his gaze fixed and staring. I didn't know about the third man. My leg pulsed with dull pain where Arsullah Hakim had stabbed me once already. I sank my fingers into the tendons and nerves of his wrist trying to force him to drop the screwdriver…

Someone was speaking to me. A calm, quiet voice cutting through the confusion and desperation, speaking right over the shots and screams—and the dream died away, faded out like someone turning down the volume.

The voice said clearly, "You're dreaming, Mark. Open your eyes."

I opened my eyes.

The reality was violet-sprigged wallpaper and soft-shaded lamplight and Stephen sitting on the edge of the bed, his silver hair ruffled, his green bathrobe gaping open to reveal the hard brown planes of his chest. Beyond him the window was open. Through the screen I could see the golden moon peeking over the sill, and beyond the gently stirring curtains, the sound of crickets.

The hushed ordinariness of it was shattering after the violent chaos of the nightmare.

"All right now?" Stephen asked, and my gaze jerked back to him.

"Storming," I managed.

He rose from the bed, went into the bathroom. I heard the taps running. My heartbeat slowed. I wiped my face. It was wet with sweat.

"That was some dream," he said, coming back into the room carrying a glass and a hand towel. His low key acceptance made it easier.

I elbowed up, wincing, and he offered a corded forearm. I grabbed on, pulling myself the rest of the way upright, taking the towel and mopping the perspiration off my face and chest. "I don't dream."

"Then you've got some unpleasant memories."

I gave him a twitchy smile and relaxed against the pillows, handing back the towel. He exchanged it for the glass of water.

"How was the concert?" I asked when I'd drained the glass. The clock next to the bed read 3:22.

"Fine. What did you dream?"

I shook my head. "I never remember my dreams."

Stephen said, "I know that's what you always said. I don't think I ever believed it."

"It's true." I started to shrug but re-thought it. "Images, impressions. That's all." If I could have had my dreams made to order, I'd have dreamed of Stephen, but I didn't even dream of him. That I knew of. There were mornings I woke up rock-hard and rarin' to go, and I always figured Stephen had played a starring role in the night's brainwaves. I said, "Sorry I woke you."

Stephen sighed. He looked tired—and he was a bloke who badly needed his sleep. "It's okay. If you're all right now —"

He turned and I got out, "Don't go."

His face closed. He said wearily, "Mark, I don't have the energy for games."

"No games," I said with an effort. "I just…don't want to be alone. If you could see your way to sleeping here tonight….I promise to stay on my side of the Mason-Dixon line."

I felt like an idiot, but even so I didn't look away. He scrubbed his face with his hand, then he studied me, hand over his mouth.

I grimaced. "I'd kip down with Lena if she were still about."

Oddly enough, that seemed to decide him. "Okay, Mason. Scoot over."

I shifted gingerly to the other side of the bed, and he turned out the lamp. I watched him, silhouetted in moonlight, as he shrugged out of his robe, threw it to the foot of the bed, and pulled the covers back, slipping into the sheets beside me, stretching out. He was wearing pajama bottoms, but I could feel his heat. He smelled familiar, a subtle musky fragrance unique to him.

I inched down in the bed, levering myself onto my side facing him—happily the side where the ribs were not broken.

His breath was light against my face. His eyes glinted in the moonlight.

“Thank you,” I said softly.

“You’re welcome,” he said equally soft, and the words seemed to take on new meaning. He held my gaze. Then he closed his eyes.

If I reached my hand out—but if I reached my hand out, he would get up and leave the room. *I love you,* I thought. I closed my eyes and went to sleep.

“I’m not the villain here.”

“You’re sure as hell not one of the guys in the white hats.”

“I’ve news for you, Stephen, not everyone wearing white is a good guy. I’ve seen burning crosses and women flogged. I’ve seen—homosexuality is a capital offense in most of the Muslim nations.”

“And you think the end justifies the means.”

“Sometimes. Yes. These things aren’t settled by knights jousting each other in tournaments, for God’s sake.”

“There’s a reason they shoot spies.”

"Fuck you, Stephen."

But he grabbed my arm before I could walk away. "That's not what I meant. Of course I don't think you're a villain. And I'm not so naïve that I can imagine a world where espionage doesn't play a major role in the balance of power. Listen, the truth is I'm scared. Scared to death every time I think about what could happen to you if you're caught and captured. You think I could survive seeing you beheaded or shot on the nightly news?"

"There's a call for you," Lena said from the back porch doorway.

I looked away from the hypnotic glitter of sunlight on the lake. "It's not Stephen?"

"It's not Doctor Thorpe. I'll bring the phone out here." She returned, handed me the phone, and eyed Buck—who was sleeping comfortably sprawled over my legs—a disapproving look.

"That dog's not supposed to be up on that swing."

I winked at her and took the phone. She gave me one of those severe looks and went back into the house.

"Yes?" I said into the receiver.

"What the hell is it you think you're up to, Mr. Hardwicke?" the Old Man snarled.

I hung up.

Then I stared in astonishment at the phone. Had I just done what I'd apparently done—or was I really losing it? Actually, in either case I appeared to be really losing it. Buck wriggled over onto his back, and balanced there braced against my jeans-clad legs, paws raised in sleeping surrender.

The phone rang again.

I answered. "Yes?"

"Don't hang up again," came the distinctly unlilting Irish accent of my employer.

I could picture the Old Man clearly. A tall, rawboned man in his sixties—fighting a valiant rearguard action against mandatory retirement—a hawkish face and a shock of unruly white hair. I always thought he looked a little like those pictures of the traitorous Anthony Blunt, but I'd never been suicidal enough to say so.

"What do you want?" I added belatedly, "Sir."

"What d'you suppose I want? Would you like to be explaining to me what the hell you're doing in the States when I expressly ordered you into hospital for rest and observation?"

I was silent trying to marshal my arguments, but in the end all I came up with was a short, "I want out."

"Out? *Out?* What the hell do you mean, you want *out*?"

"I want out. I want to retire. I told you two years ago I wanted out, and you told me that you needed me for one more job. No one else had the skills, the experience, that's what you said. And two years and eleven operations later, I'm still working for you."

There was an electric silence, and the Old Man said silkily, "That, boyo, would be because you never mentioned leaving again. There was never a word out of you when I gave you an assignment. Never a murmur."

Lunch hadn't agreed with me. Ice tea and cold chicken salad. I wasn't used to rich things like that. I was used to…rice. And yoghurt. And fruit. I felt queasy. And the heat was giving me a headache. My head pounded with it.

I focused with effort. "Well, I'm saying the word now. Two words. I'm through."

"Nonsense."

"*Nonsense?* It's not nonsense. I'm resigning."

"It is nonsense. Resigning from a job you enjoy? A job you excel at? Why?"

Because I'm tired of lying and being lied to, of betraying people and being betrayed. Tired of risking life and limb. Tired of running. Tired…

Because it cost me Stephen.

But I couldn't accept that. I said, "I'm…tired."

"Of course you're tired. That's why you're on sick leave."

"This isn't something that can be cured by sleeping tablets or a couple of weeks in Spain. I need to make a break."

"You do important work for which you are very well paid —"

"I'm not going to change my mind."

"I see." I could practically hear the gears changing. "Very well. We'll discuss it when you return."

"I'm not coming back." I closed my eyes, absently tugged Buck's silky ear. I desperately needed to lie down and sleep. Sleep away the churning in my guts, the throbbing in my head.

"You're not…?" For the first time in all the years I'd known him, the Old Man seemed truly at a loss for words. "Are you mad? What do you mean you're not coming back? Not at all? Not *ever*? What kind of childish talk is that? What about your family?"

Well, there was a silly question. My great-uncle was dead. There remained only a few scattered cousins I never heard from beyond the occasional Christmas card—received usually a month or two late when I returned from wherever I'd been last posted.

The Old Man moved on quickly, "Your friends?"

Friends? Like Barry Shelton?

"What friends? I don't have any friends. I have colleagues. I have contacts."

Next he would ask about lovers. But no. The Old Man was unlikely to make that mistake. Instead he made a sound of impatience. "What about your flat? Your car? Your book collection?"

I said nothing. What was there to say? *My book collection?* Why didn't I simply eat my pistol now?

"There are procedures, Mr. Hardwicke. You've got to follow the prescribed course of action for this kind of thing. You can't just bloody well walk out like—like someone on the television!"

Did the Old Man watch telly? I tried to picture that. Had he seen *Lord of the Rings*? He wouldn't make a half-bad wizard.

"I realize that." I said. And I did realize it. I would have to return home eventually. I had a change of jeans, a toothbrush, and a service-issued pistol. Hardly enough to build a new life on. But I didn't want a new life. I wanted my old life. The life I had passed up when I chose to go back to work instead of staying with Stephen as we'd planned.

The only problem with that plan was that Stephen no longer wanted me in his life. Which meant I had zero reason for remaining in the States. I might as well go back. Why didn't I?

"You realize what?" he said sharply when I said nothing else.

"I realize that I need to come back for a final debriefing. And I will." I rested my forehead on my hand. "But I need…"

He said nothing as my voice trailed off. When I didn't pick up the thread again, he said, "Very well. Given the injuries you sustained on your last assignment, I'll give you a little time. Forty-eight hours. But I warn you —"

I thought of the old television series with Patrick McGoohan. What was it called? *The Prisoner*, that was it.

"What?" I asked. "What will you do if I don't come back?"

He said, precise and cold as an ice pick, "I hope you never have cause to find out, Mr. Hardwicke."

Stephen's mouth on my nipple. Suckling, nibbling the tight nub. I moaned, arching up against him, and he paused in that teasing pull of teeth and lips to offer a sexy little laugh. Could you laugh with an accent? Stephen's chuckle had a soft Virginia drawl to it.

Hands sliding over his sleek hard body, stroking him, running my fingernails—such as they were—down his broad back, I tried to draw him down while my cock jutted up against his belly. Even I wasn't clear what I was urging him to do, so it was a relief when he took me in hand—literally—pumping me once, and then a second time.

I said dizzily, "Again? But what about you?"

"I'm an old man. Twice in one night is my limit."

My breath caught in my throat as his teeth closed delicately on my nipple, and I pushed into his hand.

The book slipped out of my hands and I started awake. There was a shadow standing over me, but before I could react, Stephen said, "Sorry. I didn't mean to wake you."

I relaxed into the chair, hoping he hadn't noticed that I'd been about to spring on him and knock him to the floor. I expelled a long breath. "That's all right. I don't know why I'm sleeping so much."

"It's called recovery."

"Yeah? Funny. I don't remember sleeping this much when I was shot."

He'd left for the hospital before I woke that morning, so I'd had no chance to see him since last night's dramatics. To my surprise he sat down on the footstool next to my feet and said, "We should probably go downstairs and change the dressing on your leg."

I grimaced. Then, eying the copy of the *Rubaiyat of Omar Khayyám* in his hands, I nodded at the book and said, "I'm glad you kept it."

"It's a beautiful book. And it was a gift. There's no reason not to keep it."

The inscription on the flyleaf read: One thing is certain, and the Rest is Lies.

At the time I hadn't believed there was any relevance in the rest of the quotation: *The Flower that has blown for ever dies.*

Stephen studied the blue leather cover with its gold lettering and design—and I studied Stephen: from the disarming way his hair fell soft and pale over his forehead, to that intractable square jaw. He had a sexy mouth and short, thick, dark eyelashes like a doll's. His hands were beautiful and well-cared for: long, tapered fingers equally adept at healing and giving pleasure.

He looked up, catching my gaze, and I reddened as though he could see my thoughts in a cartoon bubble over my head.

"I brought Chinese takeout for you," he said. "I have dinner plans tonight."

Disappointment closed my throat. It was ridiculous. I really was too old to feel like this. I said calmly, "Three nights in a row. Well, you've never been one to drag your feet when you see something you like."

He said tersely, "I'm not seeing Bryce. I'm having dinner with friends and then I'm attending a scholarship committee meeting at the university."

Well, that was a little relief. Not much. I urgently wanted—needed—to spend time with him. I felt sure that if we had more than a few moments on our own I might manage to open my mouth without putting my foot in. But I could see that he just as urgently wanted to avoid that very thing.

"You're very hard to say no to, did you know that?" That wry smile creasing his tanned cheek.

"The fact is, you don't really want to say no to me."

"Unfortunately you're right."

"Unfortunately?"

Even then the self-mockery in his eyes had given me pause.

I followed him downstairs to the little office and examination room where Stephen occasionally saw a few local elderly and impoverished patients. He washed his hands and dried them with a paper towel while I studied the botanical sketches on the wall.

"Is the leg giving you a lot of trouble?" His voice sounded absent.

I glanced around. "Nothing to speak of."

"And you wouldn't speak of it if it was."

"Oh well. Whinging never won wars."

"I know who that sounds like."

"Who?" I met his gaze and felt a funny flare of awareness. "The Old Man? Yes, I suppose it is one of his greatest hits."

Pulling down my jeans, I climbed carefully onto the examining table.

Stephen removed the bandage from my thigh and studied the wound. His hands were cool and dry and very gentle. I distracted myself from his touch with an effort. The injury looked all right to me. Still a little puffy and pink around the sewing but clearly healing. The tiny black stitches were so perfect a machine might have done them.

"Will I ever dance again, doctor?" I inquired as he opened a tube of antibiotic cream.

"Mercifully, no."

I laughed, and Stephen's cheek tugged into a grin. Our eyes met briefly. It was hard to look away—for me anyway. And it was hard to ignore the fact that in his effort to smear my torn thigh with antibiotic cream he was inadvertently brushing my cock with his hand.

Inevitably this began to produce results.

"Look who's awake," I remarked, since there was little hope of ignoring the tent pole in my briefs.

"Yep," Stephen agreed, glancing and then away. He continued pasting the cool cream over my sensitive inner thigh, brushing his knuckles against the hard length poking the soft cotton of my briefs—it would have been hard to miss at that point.

"That's actually a relief," I said—feeling that I had to say something. And at his blank look, I clarified, "He hasn't shown much sign of life lately."

"He hasn't?" He sounded disinterested, but his fingers lingered, his touch more caressing than medicinal. "That's common with trauma. You'll be back to normal fast enough."

"Normal" apparently not a good thing where I was concerned. I put my hand over his, holding him still against the hard large muscle of my thigh.

"Thank you for taking care of me. I don't know what I'd have —"

"Don't." He slid his hand out from under mine, and the fine hair along my thigh stood up as though brushed by static electricity.

His eyes were angry. I nodded.

Neither of us spoke as he placed a new plaster over the stitches and taped it neatly. His breath was cool and light against me, his eyelashes flickering against his cheeks as his kept his gaze on what he was doing.

"You're so goddamn lucky it didn't hit the femoral artery." His voice was low when he finally did speak.

"I know. Thanks. It does feel better." I jumped off the table—which was a mistake—and pulled my jeans back on with unsteady hands while he washed again at the little sink.

We walked back upstairs with neither of us saying anything. Shortly afterward Stephen left for his dinner, and I ate Chinese takeaway and watched the news. As usual the news was mostly bad—and that was just the surface coverage offered by the American news programs.

Inevitably pictures of Afghanistan filled the flat screen.

The bookish-looking female correspondent reported, "One person is dead and several others were wounded in Afghanistan Saturday when, according to witnesses, police opened fire on protesters accusing US-led soldiers of killing civilians."

I stared at the brown stuff in the white carton. Mongolian beef. I supposed I should be flattered that Stephen remembered I liked it, but I was no longer hungry. I headed back into the kitchen, dumped the food into Buck's dish, and put the dish out on the back porch. Opening the fridge to see what beer Stephen had, I discovered he'd got in Guinness. Tall cans of it. Not as good as at home, of course, but better than the pale ales Stephen preferred. I had a can—ignoring the little voice that sounded strangely like Stephen saying "Antibiotics and alcohol? You know better."—staring out the window over the sink at the scarlet and black-streaked skies.

The evening was long and dull. For a time I tried to read *Little Dorrit*, but for once Dickens failed to work his comfortable magic. I was too restless to concentrate, finding no pleasure in the slyly humorous but sentimental depiction of Victorian England.

“The Artful Dodger, that’s you.” But there was no sting in it. His hand rested warmly on the small of my back guiding me through the door he held open with the other.

“No. I’m David Copperfield searching for true love. I’m a romantic.”

“I’ve never met anyone less romantic than you.” He let the door to the restaurant close behind us. I glanced at his face but he was amused, slanting a knowing green look my way.

“Hey, that’s very wounding. I’ll have you kn —” I broke off as he leaned in and kissed me, his lips soft and deliberate as they pressed mine. When he released me, I said, “You don’t really care if I hold off meeting your friends for a bit, do you? Because if it really matters…”

“It doesn’t matter.”

“I’m not awfully good at small talk.”

“You’re not awfully good at big talk.” But he was laughing.

I gave up on *Little Dorrit*, got another can of Guinness from the fridge, and wandered out onto the back porch to enjoy the cool breeze and scent of magnolias. Buck had cleaned his dish of all traces of Mongolian beef. There was no sign of him, but I could hear his tags jingling in the darkness.

I had probably irretrievably bungled this from the moment I’d phoned from that drafty Devon phone box. Begging for help. Not very romantic, that. In my imagined reunions with Stephen I always showed up on his doorstep with flowers and gifts—I believe I usually wore formal evening dress—and somewhere in the distance music was playing. Lynyrd Skynyrd probably. And I always managed to say all the right things. Starting with the fact that I was sorry for letting him down so badly and that I knew he was too good for me—but that if he was willing to make allowances for abysmal stupidity, I'd spend the rest of my life making it up to him.

This imaginary Stephen was occasionally tearful and occasionally angry, but he was always forgiving. Where the hell was that bloke? Why couldn't he have a word with the real Stephen?

The truth was as the weeks—months—*years* had passed I'd exchanged the real Stephen for this dream Stephen who would always be patiently waiting for me to pull myself together and come home. The real Stephen was an intelligent, strong, sensitive man who had got tired waiting...and had found someone else. That was the simple truth, and I needed to face it. Accept it. And move on myself.

I knew it. I believed it. And yet I couldn't make myself do it.

Instead I was hanging around like some mournful ghost of love lost—one of those confused old shades who didn't yet realize he was dead.

I smothered a yawn, wondering how Stephen's meeting was going and if he would be home before I fell asleep. I usually healed quickly; even taking jet lag into consideration, my current need for so much sleep felt odd. Granted, it was a long time since I'd felt safe enough to really sleep. Maybe I was making up for lost time.

Sometime after eleven I heard Stephen's SUV in the drive. Buck came flying across the grass and up the porch steps. He stood at the porch door and whined. He looked back at me beseechingly, and I said, "He'll come. Give him a minute."

The dog and I listened to the faint vibration of the front door opening and closing—Stephen being quiet, no doubt thinking that I was tucked up in bed upstairs sleeping the deep sleep of the unjust. He moved quietly through the house, and then walked into the kitchen.

Quivering with eagerness, Buck whined at him through the screen.

You and me both, mate, I thought wryly.

"Hey, boy," Stephen said, pushing wide the screen. Buck went past him into the kitchen. Stephen stood there, his eyes searching the darkness and finding me on the old swing.

"Mark?"

"Right here."

He stepped out onto the porch, letting the door swing shut behind him, Buck hurtling back out before the door closed all the way. To my surprise, Stephen crossed to the swing and sat down beside me.

"Everything okay?"

"I just stepped out for a breath of fresh air."

I could feel him searching my face in the gloom. "Makes a change from Afghanistan, I guess."

I gave a short laugh.

He had an apple. He bit into it, chewed. The scent of apple mingled with the fragrance of the night flowers.

He handed the apple to me, and I took a bite, the taste sweet and tart on my tongue. I handed the apple back, and his fingers brushed mine, warm and familiar.

For a time we sat there watching the moonlight on the lake, listening to the lap of water. I thought of asking him how his meeting went, but it was peaceful like this and I had the illogical feeling that we were saying more in the silence than we usually managed in words—although that was probably wishful thinking.

He stirred at last, tossed the apple core over the railing into the flowerbed, and said, "You should be in bed."

"I do agree."

"Sleeping," he added.

"I sleep better when you're with me."

Nothing.

I said lightly, "I suppose you wouldn't…?"

"No. I wouldn't." Was that regret I heard in his voice?

I sighed. "Oh well. I suppose I can sleep when I'm dead."

Apparently unmoved by thoughts of my mortality, he said, "The life you lead, that probably won't be long."

I wished I could read his expression. He was just a pale blur in the shadows. I said carefully, "What if I told you I don't want to lead that life anymore."

After a pause, he said, "You told me that once before, remember? It turned out you were mistaken."

"Maybe I was just…afraid."

"I don't think so. I don't think you're afraid of much," he said.

"You'd be surprised."

"I would. Yes."

I wasn't sure what to say, but I wasn't likely to have more than one shot at this. I needed to take it. I said, "It's all I know." It was easier like this, in the darkness with Stephen just a shapeless silence on the gently creaking swing. "I've been in this game since the Old Man recruited me right out of university." I'd grown up in the service. Grown old in some ways.

"Game," he said without inflexion.

I turned my head to stare at his silhouette. "It *was* a game at first. I was nineteen. Everything's a game at nineteen. I thought it would be adventurous. Romantic. I thought it would be better than teaching history or working as a translator. The pay was certainly better."

"I know," he said. "We talked about that quite a bit as I recall." He added coolly, with that southern gentleman's drawl, "No arguing there's damn all excitement living with a country doctor."

"That's not why I went back, Stephen. It wasn't because I craved the excitement."

"No? What was it about? You needed the money?"

"It was my job." I didn't quite know what else to say. I knew how pathetic an excuse that was. "I couldn't just...quit. Not without..." Saying good-bye? Giving notice? I said, "I owed him that much."

"You owed *him?* Do you know what's weird? You never say his name. Never. It's always "the Old Man" like he's a character in a Dickens novel. Or you are."

"His name is John Holohan." No one ever referred to him as anything but the Old Man except perhaps in the Halls of Power. Granted, we were the agency everyone pretended didn't exist, so perhaps there too he went unnamed.

Stephen said, "Then you do know it. I used to wonder. I used to wonder what the hell you called him in bed."

I went very still. "That was years ago," I said finally.

"How many? Because we were years ago too."

"It was over long before I met you. Seven years ago."

He gave a short laugh.

"I'm not lying."

"I'd have to take your word for it."

I'm not sure why that hurt so much. We were both aware that I lied for a living. I guess what stung was the implication that I also lied for recreation. I took my lying rather more seriously than that.

When the time for me to answer had come and gone, Stephen said, "Do you remember how we met?"

"Of course."

I'd accompanied the Old Man to Langley to take part in a weeklong counterterrorism and integrated intelligence strategy training session for the CIA and several other intelligence agencies. I'd met Stephen at a State Department dinner. His father was a retired senator and Stephen, who had worked for a time at Walter Reed Army Medical Center, had accompanied him. I'd first spotted him across a particularly ugly centerpiece—and I thought he was beautiful in a sophisticated Cary Grant kind of way. He wore a tuxedo like it was meant to be worn, handsome and suave as he sat there listening to the speeches with that faint cynical smile. Feeling my gaze, he'd looked my way. After a long moment he smiled at me through the bonfire of candles and the forest of miniature American and British flags.

Stephen said patiently, "No, I mean, do you remember why you were there acting as liaison instead of a more senior officer?"

To some extent because I was one of the Old Man's favorites and that had been a plum assignment, but what I answered was, "I was recovering from a shooting."

"Right."

I started to get angry despite my best intentions. "I don't know what your point is, Stephen. People get hurt in my business. That wasn't why I wanted to leave the service—because I was afraid."

"That's not what I'm saying."

"What the hell *are* you saying, then? Look," I said, "I don't run out on my obligations."

"No?" He had me there. I heard the bitter satisfaction in his voice. "Were you planning on coming home this year? Next year?"

I opened my mouth but the words didn't come in time. "I —"

"That's what I thought." He rose and went into the house, letting the screen door whack shut behind him.

Chapter Five

I found him in the study putting the copy of the *Rubaiyat* back on its shelf.

"Yes," I said. "I was coming back."

Stephen looked at me appraisingly. "Well, you think you were, so I guess that's something."

"I *did* come back," I said. "I'm here. Why doesn't that count for anything with you?"

He shook his head like it was too tiring to try and explain.

"It was all—it *is* all—I'm trained to do." I said again, needing him to understand, "It's all I know."

"I realize that," he said.

Yes. He realized that. We'd talked about all this. Talked about everything. Stephen knew more about me than anyone—up to and including the agency I worked for.

"It's what you're trained for, and you're very good at it. And, assuming you don't get your head blown off, you'll probably have a long and illustrious career. The impression I received in the one real conversation I ever had with the man, was that Holohan plans on eventually grooming you for his position. Assuming you survive that long."

The thought had quite literally never occurred to me. I was struck silent.

He must have seen the surprise on my face, because he said, "Why do you think he pulled out all the stops getting you to come back?'

"I'm valuable to him."

"Yes, you are. Not only are you one of his top operatives, you're one of the only people in the world he trusts. He wasn't about to let you go without a fight." He shrugged. "And he won."

"No, he didn't," I said. "I've left the agency."

He was closing the glass-fronted bookshelf, but that got his attention. "What are you talking about?"

I hadn't intended to tell him that, but there was no turning back now. "Except…I didn't do it the way we—I'd—originally planned. I just…walked away. I'm technically AWOL, I suppose."

"You're *what*?"

"Absent Without Leave."

"I know what it means!"

"I wanted to see you. I…needed to see you."

He didn't look pleased or flattered, he looked stone-faced. "What exactly did you do?"

"After I was debriefed, after this…last time, I was supposed to report to hospital for rest and ob—treatment."

His eyes flickered.

"Instead I…I…just kept going." Clutching my Glock and my copy of *Little Dorrit*. Maybe locking me up wasn't such a bad idea.

"Why didn't you tell me this?" Definitely stone-faced. Granite.

"I was waiting for the right moment."

His brows drew together in a silver line. Finally he said, "What will happen to you?"

"I…Honestly? I don't know."

"What do you mean, you don't *know*?" He was angry again. Nothing used to ruffle him, now he was angry all the time. With me. "Are they going to come after you?"

"You mean like in the films? Or a le Carré novel? Because I know too much?" I was smiling because I thought that just *maybe* he did care a little. He didn't want to, he had convinced himself that he didn't, but on some level he had feelings for me. Of course being Stephen he'd probably be concerned for a stranger in my position too. "I'm a field agent. I know next to nothing useful. Not in the larger scheme of things."

He made an impatient gesture. We both knew that wasn't how it worked.

"I suppose I'll go on the dole with the other ex-spies."

"Christ Almighty. I don't see anything funny about this!"

It occurred to me suddenly what might really be worrying him. I said, "There won't be any trouble, Stephen. I promise you. I'll leave if things look like getting awkward."

"I'm not worried about the social scandal for God's sake." He looked like he wanted to say something else but whatever it was, he stopped himself. "I've still got political connections. I can make a few phone calls if necessary."

On my behalf or his own? I wasn't sure. I said, "I don't think it's necessary."

He didn't have an answer.

"Anyway," I said turning to leave the room—because knowing when to walk away is crucial in successful negotiation, "I wanted you to know. I was always coming back. I *did* come back."

I hoped he'd call to me, but he didn't. I left him staring after me and went upstairs.

* * * * *

Someone was in the house.

I opened my eyes staring into the darkness.

The dreams receded to a quiet distance but the conviction remained. Someone was in the house.

Rolling out of bed, I reached for the Glock and eased the magazine into the frame. I was across the floor in two steps, back pressed to the wall next to the door. I listened, took a quick glance around the door frame, and moved into the hall, taking shelter behind the antique steamer trunk along the wall. The door to Stephen's room was closed.

Good. I wanted him well out of the action. Safe.

I listened. Someone was moving downstairs—someone was going through papers. I could hear the faint scrape and rustle…

Slowly, softly, I pulled the slide back on the Glock, chambering a bullet. I rose from my crouch behind the trunk and moved down the hallway. As I soft-footed toward the head of the stairs, a rug rose up out of the darkness at my feet—a rug that turned out to be twenty-four inches tall, furry, warm and alive. I tripped and went sprawling, my finger instinctively tightened on the Glock's trigger and I heard the oval mirror on the first landing shatter as a shot blasted through the night.

Buck began to bark. Stephen's door flew open and the landing light came on as I was pulling myself to my feet with the help of the banister railing.

"*Mark?* Jesus Christ! What the hell is happening now?" He strode down the hallway toward me—barefoot, navy pajama bottoms, unarmed—shocked eyes taking in the shattered glass, the barking dog, and me.

"I think there's someone in the house." I started hobbling down the staircase, and nearly fell over Buck again as he charged ahead of me.

That kind of thing simply didn't occur in the field. Frankly, nothing like this had occurred to me in a decade worth of field work. I caught myself from tumbling headlong. Stephen grabbed my other arm.

"What are you trying to do? Where do you think you're going?"

I yanked away and, for an incredible third time, nearly fell over the bloody damned dog galloping back *up* the stairs. The only thing that saved me from pitching forward that time was Stephen's hasty grab for my shoulder.

And all at once the adrenaline drained away, leaving me weaving slightly with bewilderment and fatigue. The dog would not be racing up and down the staircase if someone was actually in the house. Despite Buck's poor taste in liking me, he actually was a pretty good watchdog, and belatedly it dawned on me that he would not have slept through a break-in that was loud enough to wake me.

"I-I…"

Steven was staring at me like he suspected I might detonate. He had my shoulder in that hard, restraining hold. All at once my various aches and pains—and a few new ones—came rushing back.

"Sit down for a second," he ordered, and I did, folding up on the stairs, resting my arms on my knees and my head on my arms. Stephen loosened the Glock from my hand, and I didn't resist.

Was I going insane? What the fuck was the matter with me?

The dog's breath was hot on my arms. He snuffled my hair.

"Get away, Buck."

Stephen rested his hand on the back of my neck. I jumped, then relaxed as he gently kneaded my knotted muscles.

"I thought someone was in the house," I said, muffled.

"Yes, I…er…gathered that." There was no anger in his voice now.

"I could hear them going through your papers…"

We were both silent, and into the silence came the scrape of fluttering papers. I raised my head, and Stephen said—a little guiltily—"I probably left the fans on downstairs. I do that sometimes. It's moving the newspaper around."

I nodded, pressed the heels of my hands to my eyes. He continued to stroke my neck and shoulders.

"Sorry about the mirror."

He actually sounded amused as he said, "I never liked it anyway. I thought it emphasized the bags under my eyes."

Neither of us said anything for a time.

"What do you think is the matter with me?" I didn't dare take my hands down, didn't dare look at him.

"I think you're suffering from nervous exhaustion. Maybe traumatic stress," he replied calmly. "What do you think is wrong with you?"

I thought that over. Could it be something that simple?

"I'm afraid I'm one of those people who can't adjust to…civilian life."

"Do you really want to?"

I nodded.

He sounded indulgent, like he was humoring me. "Yeah? What would you like to do with the rest of your life?"

I managed to joke, "Besides spend it with you?" I risked a look at him.

He actually smiled back. "Besides that."

"I don't know. Write a big, bestselling roman à clef based on my brilliant career."

He was quiet for a moment. "You talked about teaching. Before."

Before. Two years before when we had been planning to build a life together.

"I'd like to teach, yeah."

"Why don't you think about how you could make that happen?" His hand stroked down my spine and I shivered.

If I had never met the Old Man, if I hadn't allowed myself to be lured away from the dull safety of academia by the promise of adventure and romance like a right prat in the *Oxford Book of Adventure Stories* I'd have followed in my great-uncle's footsteps with a fellowship at some quiet little university. I wouldn't have been shot or stabbed. I wouldn't have watched a woman immolate herself in a market square or seen children blown to pieces by a car bomb.

I'd never have met Stephen.

"Let's get you back in bed," he said, and obediently I rose and climbed back up the stairs with his help.

* * * * *

He ejected the magazine and laid the Glock back on the stand. I met his eyes.

"I am sorry about the mirror. I know it was an antique." I inched painfully down in the bed. "I'll pay for it, naturally."

He had stepped into the bathroom. He returned with a glass of water and a couple of pain pills—at least I thought they were pain pills. I wouldn't have blamed him for knocking me out for the rest of the night. He said, "Forget about the mirror. Everything in this place is an antique. Including me."

I snorted. Tossed the pills back, washed them down, and got over onto my good side, pausing as a spasm caught me off guard.

"All right?"

I nodded quickly. The little thrill of anguish faded and I eased down. It was better once I was lying flat. I said tentatively, "Will you stay for a bit? Just till I drop off?"

He barely hesitated. "If you'd like."

"I'd like." I sighed. "I'd like it every night for the rest of my life."

He didn't respond to that, but he went ahead and climbed into bed and I reached for him. He gathered me against him and it felt easy and natural—and right. He held me for a bit and then said, "How are the ribs?"

"Hurting like hell."

I felt him smiling against my hair. "I bet. We could try lying —"

"I don't care. It's worth it." And it *was* worth the ache of knitting bones and muscles to lie like this, to have the freedom to rest my head on the warmth of his bare shoulder, feeling the steady thump of his heart against my own, feeling his breath warm and even against my face. His arms were hard and muscular but they seemed to cradle me.

He said quite kindly, “You’ll get over it, Mark.”

I thought about not answering, but I said finally, “You may be right about my ribs, but you don’t know a damn thing about my heart.”

He didn’t say anything.

After a time the pain pills kicked in and my ribs didn’t hurt so much despite the awkward position. Stephen’s body was relaxed but I could feel him awake, feel him thinking. I wondered what his thoughts were, but it no longer seemed crucial to know. Somehow in the long stretch of silence I felt we had reached some kind of truce, even a sort of understanding.

I said softly, “I think I might be losing it.”

He considered it. Said equally soft, “You might have temporarily mislaid it. I don’t think you’ve lost it.” The smile in his voice was reassuring. I believed him.

Then Buck, curled up on the floor somewhere beyond the foot of the bed, suddenly groaned in that exasperated way dogs do, and we both chuckled.

Dawn was scented of the lilacs that grew along the back of the house. For a time I lay there watching the first fingers of sunlight reach through the curtains, stretch across the ceiling. I listened to Stephen breathing softly beside me. The soft rosy light reminded me of the artwork in the copy of the *Rubaiyat of Omar Khayyam*—the first gift I had given him.

He had hated what I did for a living. He didn't pretend for the sake of politeness—not even in the very beginning. But I liked that about him. I liked his blunt honesty. It was unknown in my trade. With Stephen it wasn't about politics—although it bothered him that it wasn't about politics for me either—he was a doctor and he saw what was happening in the Middle East purely from the humanitarian standpoint. He saw war—all war—as a terrible tragedy.

And he was right, of course. But it did seem a little beside the point.

Even once I had decided to leave the service we still rowed about it. About war, about espionage, about the Middle East itself.

I wasn't sure where my own fascination with the Middle East stemmed from. One too many readings of the *Jungle Book*? I vividly remembered flipping through the lush illustrations of my great-uncle's copy of the *Rubaiyat*. I had been nine—not long after the death of my parents in a plane crash. My great-uncle David, a Fellow at Grey College, was my only close relative, and I had gone to live with him.

"Two old confirmed bachelors, that's us, my boy," he'd used to say cheerfully.

He died when I was eighteen.

He had a sumptuous collection of Asian and Middle Eastern art books and literature. But it was the *Rubaiyat* with those astonishing watercolors by Edmund Dulac that had first caught my attention, opening a doorway into another world. A world of romance and adventure and mysticism. A land of white peacocks and moonlit temples and secret gardens and princely men in turbans. Granted, by the time I'd been recruited by the Old Man I wasn't stupid enough to imagine that was the way it really was, but combined with my adolescent fondness for Ian Fleming, I suppose I was a natural recruit for the latest version of The Great Game—and an eventual posting in the Land of Light.

And some of it had been just as I imagined. The land—the part that wasn't blasted to bits—was starkly beautiful and strange like any fairytale landscape, the people were as alien as characters in ancient legends, and the history fascinated me—but that was where the magic ended. Violence, deceit, betrayal...that was the coin of the realm.

And yet...

Until Stephen it had not seriously entered my mind that I could walk away from it. Not even after I'd been shot in a botched operation in Calcutta. What was there to walk away for?

I was distracted by the feel of Stephen's morning erection prodding my belly; I'd been up and awake for some little while myself. I smiled inwardly, nestling closer, fitting my hips to his, moving carefully against him. I could feel his heat through the thin cotton of his pajama bottoms.

His breathing changed as his cock swelled and filled, shoving its way through the fly of the constraining pajamas. I bumped my hips against his in soft, stealthy movements that might weave themselves into his dream—or not.

He mumbled something sleepy and opened his eyes.

I smiled into his sleep-hazed green eyes, and he smiled back—and it was just like old times. There was happiness in his eyes and his mouth found mine in a sweet, sleepy kiss. He tasted smoky, like a darker version of himself. I fingered the mussed silver of his hair, running my hand down his bristling cheek, a cheek flushed and pink as a boy's.

He closed his eyes again. Maybe he thought he was dreaming. If so, I didn't want to spoil it by saying a wrong word. I kissed him again and slipped my tongue into his mouth, touching his tongue delicately with my own. He made an approving noise. His tongue swirled lazily around mine.

It was killing my ribs to hold my arm up, but I stroked the silky soft hair on the nape, resting my hand on the back of his neck, drawing him closer, deepening the kiss. I slipped my other hand inside his pajama fly, finding and holding the velvety softness of his balls. He touched me back, and I sighed my pleasure as he ran a slow hand down my torso, light as a feather over the taping on my ribs, then smoothing his palm over my abdomen.

"Rub my belly for good luck," I whispered.

He smiled, not opening his eyes, and gently rubbed his hand across my navel.

“Now make a wish,” I told him inaudibly, and kissed him.

His hand slowly slid down till his fingers tangled in the pubic hair where my cock nested. I murmured encouragingly into his mouth.

Languidly, we caressed and stroked each other. So drowsily intimate, smelling pleasurably of the clean linen and our warm bodies. Reaching beneath the bedclothes, he freed himself from his pajama bottoms. And I hurried to follow suit, painfully wriggling out of my briefs—and that was lovely: bare naked skin finding bare naked skin.

He slid his hands beneath me easing me over onto my back, and I liked his strength and his carefulness, though I didn’t need him to be careful. I felt fine. Better than fine. I smiled up at him and his eyes were open. He wasn’t smiling; his lashes shadowed his gaze, but there was something tender in the serious line of his mouth.

I let my legs fall open as he leaned over me, hands planted on either side of my shoulders, cock brushing mine but his weight off my body, the sheets and cover tenting over us.

“It’s okay,” I whispered, running my hands down the smooth skin of his ribcage and flanks. I reached up, cupping his taut buttocks with my hands, inviting him to settle on top of me. He resisted. “I want you to.”

“Shhh,” he said, and I shushed as his warm mouth found my throat, trailing moist kisses down to my collarbone and finally closing over my nipple right above the stiff taping around my ribs.

I sucked in a sharp breath, half pleasure, half pain as I made the mistake of arching against the feel of that mouth on puckered skin. Our cocks rubbed against each other, stiff and velvety and slick all at the same time.

The moving finger writes, I thought as Stephen’s prick inked a salty message against my abdomen and groin. My own cock slid against his, penning an urgent answer. I thrust up against him, biting back frustration as the reminding twinges of various cuts and bruises and breaks made themselves felt.

“Shush now,” he murmured.

And despite wanting his weight on me, pressing me down into the pillowy softness of the feather mattress, despite wanting our bodies locked together in heat and hunger, I sealed my lips. This felt very good, that delicious friction as he rocked against me, our cocks thrusting and scraping against each other despite the fact that it had a distant dreamy quality to it. I found it hard to believe that Stephen and I were really lying there fucking, and yet at the same time it had a sense of inevitability.

Slowly, relentlessly, tension built to that unbearable peak and then suddenly that spurt of wet warmth, a fountain of delight spilling out of me in dulcet pulses. Splashing his groin and belly, splashing my thighs. Lovely, loose release murmuring through my nerves and muscles and bones.

Poised above me, Stephen shivered down the length of his body, hips freezing. He bit off a sound, shot thick cream across my belly and chest, sharply pungent with his essence.

His left arm gave way, then his right, and his body lowered solidly onto mine. He panted into my ear and hair, and I wrapped my arms around him, holding him in place when he'd have lifted off me. My heart thudded in slow, happy time with the beat of his. I closed my eyes savoring it, treasuring that moment, wanting it to last forever. I hoped he wouldn't regret it.

And having writ, moves on. Nor all your Piety nor Wit shall lure it back to cancel half a line…

"I'm hurting you," he muttered after a bit, trying to lift off again. I hung on, knowing he would have to permit it. He wouldn't risk wrestling with me.

"Then we're even," I whispered. I felt the tension in his body but couldn't have stopped the words if my life had depended on it. After a heartbeat or two he relaxed.

We drifted while the sunshine spread across the floorboards. After a time I came back to alertness and realized Stephen was easing off me. I let him go reluctantly, relieved when he lowered himself beside me, wrapped his arm around my middle, and went to sleep. I closed my eyes and drowsed, content—even confident that everything would be okay.

Nor all your Tears wash out a Word of it.

Lulled, I closed my eyes. I felt him rise an hour later, easing off the mattress. The dog followed him out of the room, nails clicking on the hardwood floor. I heard the old plumbing rattle, and a short time later the house settled back into sleep.

Chapter Six

.

I was having breakfast—French toast with red raspberry sauce—when the phone rang. I watched Lena answer it, watched her eyes slide my way. I felt certain it was something I wasn't going to like—although after the start my morning had had, I felt it would take a lot to ruin it.

"It's a Mr. Holohan for you," she said at last, holding the phone up.

For a beat I couldn't think who Mr. Holohan was. Then I said, "Tell him I'm not here."

She was shaking her head—not entirely regretful to give me bad news. "He said you would say that. He said he has to talk to you. It's urgent."

I rose, taking the phone with a sound of impatience, and went out on the back porch.

"You said I had forty-eight hours."

The Old Man snarled, "Oh for God's sake, man. Forty-eight hours is nearly up!"

"No it's not. I've got…" I looked at my wristwatch, calculating.

He snapped, "Mr. Hardwicke, our prior arrangement is rescinded. You're to come in now."

"You can't arbitrarily rescind —" He could of course, and frequently did, but my rage was chilled by his next words.

"Listen very carefully. This morning the Cousins raided an illegal embassy in Kunar. Your name was discovered on a hit list of enemies of the Taliban."

In the following silence, I could hear Buck in the distance barking at something in that mechanical, repetitious way dogs do when they can't remember what got them started in the first place.

I said when I could think clearly, "*My* name? My actual name? Why the hell should my name be on anything? I'm just —"

"Think, man. Use your head. Arsullah Hakim was the younger brother of Mullah Arsullah."

It rocked me. Mullah Arsullah was a senior Taliban commander. I said after some rapid thinking, "Still. What are the odds? I've left Afghanistan and I won't be back. And even if they're hunting me, why should they look for me here? And if they did…"

They had my real name. It was, admittedly, a shock.

"The Istakhbarat has operatives looking for you. There's a price on your head. One million rupees."

"There is no Istakhbarat," I argued. The Istakhbarat was Afghanistan's former intelligence agency under the Taliban regime. Officially there was no Istakhbarat. Unofficially… "Anyway," I swallowed hard. "A million rupees. What's that work out to, about fifty quid?"

He said flatly, "It's over two hundred thousand American dollars. But that's merely added incentive. Killing you is a matter of honor. A matter of pride. You must come in now."

"I've still got twenty hours," I said.

"Oh, for God's sake, Mark," the Old Man said. "Is it worth your life?"

"It might be." I heard the words and realized I meant them.

He argued of course, but even he had to admit the odds were against terrorists tracking me to this small corner of the Shenandoah Valley.

"Are you willing to take the chance with Thorpe's life?" the Old Man asked finally, unanswerably.

"You've said yourself the chances of my being found here are practically nonexistent."

"Then you're willing to take that chance? You're willing to risk his life?"

I was silent. If I left now, I knew it would be over. Stephen wouldn't believe such a melodramatic reason for my pulling out, and even if he did, it wouldn't matter because I had screwed up too many times. I was out of chances. I might not even have a chance now, although it had certainly felt this morning that I did.

"You know damn well I'm not," I said bitterly. "I'll phone you this evening and set up when I'm coming in."

* * * * *

Despite the phone call, I felt better that morning than I had for days. I was finally able to stay awake for more than an hour or two, and I spent the morning checking out teaching programs at local universities. I told myself I was just curious. Then I told myself that even if I did have to leave for a time I could convince Stephen to…

To what?

Each time my thoughts sheered off like a low flying plane narrowly avoiding treetops. I concentrated instead on the different websites and the wealth of information offered.

The University of Shenandoah had something called a Career Switcher Program for individuals who hadn't completed teacher training curriculum but had "considerable life experiences, career achievements, and academic backgrounds that are relevant." I had considerable life experiences, and a decade of survival in my business was quite a career achievement, but was any of it relevant?

I was well paid and I'd saved a considerable amount over the years. Other than having acquired a number of first editions of Dickens, I didn't spend a lot—even on the rare occasions I'd been home for any length of time. I could afford to go back to university and get a proper teaching degree. And I liked the idea of teaching, especially of teaching history. It hadn't been something I'd said because I thought Stephen wanted to hear it.

If I could find some place local…

There were all kinds of colleges and universities. Blue Ridge Community College, Southern Virginia University, James Madison University. I studied pictures of brick buildings and smiling young faces and tried to tell myself it wasn't too late. I could do this. People went back to school all the time.

I could start school in the fall—if Stephen liked the idea. If Stephen was willing to give me another chance.

A little before lunch time I had a surprise visitor: Bryce Boxer.

"Stephen's not here," I said after Lena showed him into the study where I was surfing the Web on Stephen's desktop and making copious notes on courses of study and prerequisites, tuition, and fees.

Bryce approached the desk, and I clicked to reduce the screen. His blue eyes met mine, and I could read the suspicion there. What did he imagine? Credit card fraud? Chat room scams with underage boys? It was obvious he didn't have the details of why Stephen and I had broken up, but he saw me as the bad guy.

Granted, I *was* the bad guy.

He said, gaze returning to my face, "Yeah, I know. I wanted to…speak frankly to you. Man-to-man."

Queen, I thought. I said politely, "Go ahead."

He picked up the Civil War cast iron rifle piece that Stephen used as a paperweight and then put it down again. He seemed to have trouble coming to it. I pushed back in the chair, folded my arms, waiting.

He said abruptly, "I know exactly four things about you, Mark. You like Dickens, Guinness, dogs, and French toast."

I raised my brows.

He said, "Make that five. You broke Stevie's heart. What else should I know?"

I could tell you but I'd have to kill you.

Why would Stephen want to be with someone like this? I said, "I like classical music and I took a first in oriental studies at Cambridge. What else do you think you need to know?"

"How long did you plan on staying?" he asked bluntly.

"That's up to Stephen. I'd like to stay permanently. Why?"

Apparently the man-to-man thing wasn't supposed to be quite that frank. "S-s-stay?" he stuttered. "You can't *stay*!"

"Why?"

"*Why*? Because…because it's over between you. It's ended. Finished."

I shrugged. "Things change."

"Those things don't change. And you know why? Very honestly? Because your being here makes Stevie unhappy."

Stevie.

My lip curled. "Unhappier than when I'm away?"

"Yes! These days, yes."

I smiled, deliberately provoking. "I shall have to work on that."

"You arrogant shit!"

I raised an eyebrow. I wanted him to come after me. Try to hit me with the Civil War relic or take a swing at me. Something. I hadn't quite decided what I would do if he did. The best thing would be to let him knock me down. That would put him squarely in the wrong with *Stevie*. But I wasn't sure I had the discipline to do it. I so dearly wanted to smash his face in.

But either his self-control was better than mine or I didn't look nearly as unthreatening as I believed. He didn't make a move my way—choosing instead to keep flapping his mouth.

"Do you care about Stephen at all? Or are you just using him again?"

I consciously forced my hands to unknot, relax. It didn't matter what this prick thought. I didn't need to justify myself to him. Stephen's opinion was the only one that mattered. Stephen didn't think I had used him. He couldn't think that. Stephen knew I had loved him. This was all Brent. I said coolly, "What do you care?"

Brent's mouth worked. I thought he might even cry. He said, "Because I love him. Because he's starting to love me back. Because we could have something good together if you don't destroy it—just because you can."

In two steps I could be out of that chair and across the floor. In two steps—approximately four seconds—I could snap his neck. It would be easy. A pleasure. But I wouldn't. I wouldn't harm even one of the remaining hairs on his head.

Because without meaning to he'd told me what I most wanted to hear.

* * * * *

But of course, proof of how little I understand the way these things work: I won the battle but lost the war.

Stephen arrived home early as I was e-mailing off requests for information and school brochures. My smile faded as I saw his face. Back to square one, it seemed. He had looked more pleased to see me the day I arrived bloodstained and dazed at the airport a very long time ago.

He said furiously, "What the hell did you say to Bryce?"

I admit I hadn't thought Bryce would run straight to him. Not only did it indicate a level of trust and understanding between them that I hadn't been counting on, it was embarrassing to be caught squabbling over him like a pair of adolescent queens.

I said slowly, confusedly absorbing just how angry he was, "But Brent attacked me."

"*Bryce*," he shot back. "And *what* in God's name can *possibly* be going on in that scrambled brain of yours? He *attacked* you? How the hell did he attack you? Do you know what an attack is? Do you understand the concept of disagreeing with someone without having to destroy them? *Jesus Christ,* Mark. You don't...you don't use nuclear weapons on white mice."

I had never seen him like this. He looked like he hated me. I tried to think back to the scene with Brent—Bryce. Surely he was the aggressor there? I had gone for his weak spot, yes, but...he had gone for mine, hadn't he? And wasn't the deck already stacked in his favor?

With a sick pang I realized what Stephen was saying. He *loved* Bryce. When I hurt Bryce I hurt Stephen because…Bryce was the one Stephen wanted. Not me.

I blinked, trying to comprehend this as Stephen went on in that deep, ferocious voice. "I didn't want you here. I let you come against my better judgment. I specifically told you that you had no rights here. That there was no longer anything between us." That was a little harsh even for Stephen. He must have heard it—or perhaps read it in my face. He qualified tersely, "Other than friendship. And this is not the way friends behave. You've deeply hurt someone I care about."

Well that was plain enough, even for me. I tried to keep all emotion out of my voice. "He wanted to know when I was leaving—as I seem to be getting in his way."

His eyes narrowed. "And what did you tell him?"

"That it wasn't any of his business."

He paused, possibly to consider his words, and then he said quietly, no room for misunderstanding, "And when exactly *are* you leaving, Mark?"

I considered the possibility that he was asking because he was actually afraid of my going, but reluctantly let the idea go. It was clear from his expression that he wasn't anything but impatient to see the last of me.

It took a second to face it, but then I was all right again. I hadn't really believed this was going to work out, had I? Surely I wasn't that naïve? That…romantic? That goddamned, bloody stupid? I pressed "cancel" on the email I had been about to send.

I said, "It seems I'm leaving tonight."

And it made perfect sense. Better for me, really. And not least because I might have one or two representatives from the psychopath community hunting me—not to mention the embarrassing possibility of the Old Man arranging a courtesy call from the Cousins on my behalf. Wouldn't Stephen love that? The CIA showing up on his front porch?

"Would you like me to talk to Bryce?" I offered. "I could…" I could what? Explain that I wasn't quite sane when it came to Stephen? Maybe not quite sane period.

"You must be joking. You've said plenty already."

I nodded.

Stephen's anger seemed to fade away. He said more calmly, "I'm not saying you need to leave tonight. Or even tomorrow. So long as we're clear —"

"Crystal," I assured him. I dredged up what I hoped was a reassuring smile. "And don't worry. I didn't say anything to Bre…Bryce about last night. This morning, rather."

He winced. "Mark, this morning was —"

I couldn't bear hearing him say it was a mistake. "No, I realize that. I'm not such a fool that I think it was anything but what it was. Sex. Lovely sex at that."

He didn't return my smile. He looked like he was in pain. Well, that would be his oversensitive conscience. He'd have to work that one out on his own. I nodded at the computer and said, "I should have asked first. Is it all right if I use this to look up flights?"

"Of course." He said a little irritably, "But I've already told you you don't need to worry about it for a day or two."

"No worries." I turned back to the screen and clicking automatically. British Airways came up filling the screen.

I could feel him hesitating. I wished he would go away. What did he want from me? I kept tapping the keyboard and at last he turned and left me to it.

Once his footsteps had died away down the hall, I let my hands fall to my lap and I closed my eyes. I was so…tired…

"I love you." His green eyes were soft and serious.

I opened my mouth, but nothing came out.

"Too soon?" And he was actually smiling—smiling—as though he understood completely. And of course he didn't. How could he?

My eyes stung. I blinked hard and said gruffly, "God no." I put my arms around him so he couldn't see what a fool I was. I said against his ear, "I love you too. I always will."

Lena's voice said crisply, shattering my numb solitude, "Personally? I don't care if you go drown yourself in that big old

Atlantic Ocean. I think Mr. St—Dr. Thorpe could do a lot better than you. I think he deserves a lot better than someone like you."

I opened my eyes and looked at her. "Are you just saying this to cheer me up?"

Her mouth tightened, but she went on anyway. "But for two years that man hung on—*two years*—waiting for you to pull your head out of—"

She caught herself. I said politely, "The clouds?"

"And when it ended—when you told him whatever it was you told him—I thought he would die of grief."

"People don't die of grief."

"Honey, when you've been around as long as me, you can tell me what people do and don't do." She studied me. "I've known Dr. Thorpe since he was a boy, and he's always known who he was and what he wanted. When the Senator tried to pressure him to go into politics, he stuck to his guns. And that took some doing. And when his mother, bless her heart, wanted him to marry and give her a grandchild, he was just as gentle as he could be, but he told her the truth."

I said, "Yes, he's very good at saying no. No room for misunderstanding."

She made a noise…it sounded something like *Tchaw*! "You feel mighty sorry for yourself, don't you?"

I thought it over. "Not yet. It's not real to me yet. Mostly I feel blank."

She blinked. Her next words were brisk, but there was something different in her tone. “I’ve known that man his entire adult life, and the happiest he ever was, was with you. It’s not over for him. I heard some of what he said, and I guess he wishes it were true, but he still —” She took a deep breath. “He still loves you. And I don’t think, whatever he says, that he really wants you to leave.”

There wasn’t much to pack. There never was. I traveled light. Always. He travels fastest who travels alone—and I preferred traveling alone, really. It was much safer that way. Safer for everyone. I stuffed my copy of *Little Dorrit* into my bag and thought about Barry Shelton. We’d entered Afghanistan four months ago traveling mostly on foot from the Pakistani border city of Quetta across the straight and rigid white mountains that lined the frontier and, sticking to tracks too rough and remote for anything but mountains goats and bandits, journeying far into the rugged hills of the central Oruzgan province—and from there to Khandahar.

I’d liked Barry. I hadn’t loved him. We were partners. Mates. It had nothing to do with the way I felt about Stephen. I’d never felt for anyone the way I felt for Stephen. But we’d made a good team, Barry and I. And there had been a few nights that we’d offered each other affection and comfort, and it had been good. It had kept us strong. Kept us sane.

It hadn't felt like a betrayal, because…at that point there was nothing left to betray. Stephen had broken it off with me. Although, if I was honest with myself, I never believed for an instant that I couldn't mend that bridge. Needed to believe it. Because Stephen was my talisman, and his love for me was the dreamcatcher—the shining bit of improbability that kept away the darkest moments. When the job was over I planned to find him, apologize, explain, woo and win him back. I had it all planned. That was all right with Barry. Not that we talked about it. But he had a girl waiting for him. *Chloe Scratchett.* I didn't think I would ever forget her name. It sounded so Dickensian. Or perhaps like a porn star. He used to ramble on about her all the time.

I packed my bag and sat on the edge of the bed in Stephen's guestroom, and a wave of tiredness hit me. I wanted to lie down and close my eyes, close everything out. But now I knew what it was. Nervous exhaustion. And what was that except being afraid to face facts?

So I forced myself off the bed and went downstairs.

I found him in the kitchen staring out the window over the sink. I made sure he heard me coming, stepped on the third floorboard from the doorframe, the board that always squeaked, but he didn't move, didn't turn.

I said, wanting to make this easy for him, "My flight from Dulles is scheduled for tomorrow at fourteen hundred which means I had to book a flight from Norfolk for nine —" His expression, as he turned from staring out the kitchen window, gave me pause. I said, "If you'd like me to get a taxi —"

Stephen said, "I don't want you to get a taxi. I'll take you to the airport."

"You don't have to. It means getting up at the crack of dawn. I'd just as soon —"

"I said I would take you." He stared back out the window.

"All right. Thank you."

Nothing.

I studied the tense line of his back, and then I thought…may as well be hanged for a sheep as a lamb. I moved behind him, slipped my arms around his waist. He stiffened instantly. I rested my head against the back of his. His hair was silk against my face.

For a moment he let me stay like that. I felt the fast, steady thump of his heart next to mine. Excited. Not angry, not alarmed. He liked this too. But he didn't want to, and that made all the difference.

"I love you," I said quietly.

He shook his head.

I kept talking. What did I have to lose now? Nothing. And I owed him this much. Owed him for those two years when he had hung on, holding the door open for me, offering me safe passage if I'd just been able to see it. "I know you don't want to hear it. I know it's too late."

"It *is* too late." There was regret in his tone, but certainty.

"The mistakes I made—they didn't have to do with anything but being afraid. I did love you. I do love you."

"Don't." He pulled away. Not roughly. Without haste—or reluctance. "There's no point to this now." His eyes were very green—brilliant—but the tears were for the waste of it.

"Can I just say it anyway? For the record?"

"What's the use?"

"I don't know. Confession is good for the soul? And mine needs all the help it can get?"

His expression turned sardonic. "So it's really about you."

"This part is."

He waited.

I said, "It's the oldest story in the world. I got scared. You offered me everything I ever wanted—just like that. Mine for the taking. And it frightened the hell out of me. I didn't see how it could be…true."

"You should have stayed long enough to find out."

"I should have. Yes. I always meant to come back, but—this is the part that's hard to explain, the part you won't understand—after a time the dream of it, the promise of it became too important to…test."

Zero comprehension on his face.

I took a deep breath. I was so very bad at this kind of thing, but if I was ever going to explain myself properly, now was the time. "These last few days have given me time to think it through. My life, personally, professionally…it's about lies and deceit and betrayal and treachery. Since I was nineteen. It's my job to persuade people to trust me, and then I use them. Sometimes I betray them. Even if I don't personally betray them, I know that they will be betrayed. I lie to people. I trick them. I get them to turn on each other, sell each other out. I've always believed it was for a good cause, but mostly…it's my job." At his expression, I said, "I'm not excusing it, just trying to explain. So you'll understand that it wasn't…you."

"I know damn well it wasn't me."

"Right. Well." I shrugged. "It sounds feeble, I realize. I don't have…a great opinion of human nature."

"Are you trying to say you didn't trust me?" Stephen inquired.

"I'm trying to say I was too afraid to find out. That having the dream of you and this place was better—seemed safer, anyway—than finding out that it wasn't true."

He shook his head. "That's sad. I don't know what else to tell you. It's one of the saddest things I ever heard. Because it was all here for you. All you ever had to do was reach for it."

"I know." And I knew I could never make him understand how terrifying it was to be offered your dream.

Stephen said, "I waited two years for you to make up your mind. There was always one last job, one last crisis, one final commitment, and you kept drifting further and further away. The last time we talked—before you went to Afghanistan—I was talking to a stranger."

I thought of all the times he had needed me, wanted me: his father's death, his fiftieth birthday, changing jobs—and all the long days and lonely nights in between.

I said, "Maybe it seemed that way, but I was coming back. I knew after we talked the last time, after you broke it off, that I'd made a mistake. That I couldn't lose you. I told Barry —"

"Barry?" he interjected politely.

I hesitated. I didn't want secrets between us, but now was not the time to try and explain about Barry. "A fellow agent—a friend. I told him, right before things went…wrong…that I'd worked out what I wanted."

"How nice for you."

Once again I'd managed to say the wrong thing. I stared at Stephen's impassive face, saw the coolness in his eyes, and knew that I'd managed to confirm his decision that I was not someone he wanted or needed in his life.

I said, "I realize that it's over for you. That for you it's been over for some time. All I wanted to say was that I did love you. Still do love you. Can't imagine ever not loving you. And I'm sorry. Truly sorry. And I hope you'll forgive me for wasting two years of your life."

A muscle moved in his jaw. I could see him weighing it, deciding whether he would accept it at face value or not. He said finally, "Thank you. I know that wasn't easy for you."

And that was it. What had I expected? It was over.

Chapter Seven

"I'll be gone for about an hour, but I'll be home for supper," Stephen said from the porch.

I tossed the ball one last time to Buck and glanced back. I'd heard the phone jangle a few minutes before, and I knew who he was going to see. Bryce would, not unnaturally, want a full accounting.

"Not to worry," I replied. "And no need to rush home. I'll probably have an early night." And I probably would. Tomorrow was going to be a long day.

"Up to you," he said indifferently.

When I looked back he was gone from the porch.

I threw the ball a few more times to Buck, but he found my efforts disappointing and eventually wandered off to harass the waterfowl.

I watched the sunset for a time, then went inside the house. It seemed unnaturally quiet. Lena had left for the day shortly after her pep talk to me—kindly meant but clearly off-mark. I made myself tea, found some oatmeal biscuits in the cupboard, and went into Stephen's study to phone the Old Man.

I caught him on his way out for a late supper for some Minister or another. I told him I was coming in, and gave him the details. He was surprisingly cordial—but then he was always gracious in victory and relentless in defeat.

"I'll be letting our associates at Langley know," he said.

"I don't need a babysitter," I said. "I can get myself home without an escort."

"All the same," he said. And I shut up. Of course I would have a CIA escort—certainly until I got on the plane, and maybe all the way across the shining sea. That was mere professional courtesy. I had broken protocol, violated a dozen policies. Having my flight changed to one of the chartered CIA specials was the least of it. I was looking at a psych evaluation and a probable sanction. I might even be out of a job, but that was probably too much to hope for.

I said, "Then can we set the pick up for Dulles?" I didn't want to be taken into custody in front of Stephen.

The Old Man hesitated, but he was a shrewd old bird and I think he knew exactly what my problem was—and of course the more I cooperated, the happier everyone would be.

He agreed, told me urbanely he looked forward to seeing me, and rang off. I turned on the TV, watched for a time. Was there anywhere in the world that wasn't a mess?

An hour went by.

Then another.

It was dark outside and the crickets were chirping—and there was no sign of Stephen.

Not totally unexpected. In Bryce's shoes I'd have been equally reluctant to trust me. Nor would Stephen be looking forward to an evening of my company should I not be tactful enough to take myself off to bed early.

Another hour passed.

I must have dozed. When I opened my eyes I heard Buck barking, and I knew that bark. I'd heard it outside mountain villages and inside the walls of a private estate. I knew it because I was usually the cause of it. The barking grew louder and then I heard Stephen's SUV in the front drive, tires crunching on gravel.

The floorboard near the kitchen creaked.

And all at once I knew we were in a hell of a mess.

I turned out the lamp and rolled off the sofa onto the floor. Footsteps vibrated down the hall toward the study. I skittered over to the rifle cabinet, but it was locked. Probably no one had opened it since the Senator died.

Diving behind Stephen's desk, I grabbed the heavy cast iron paperweight. The overhead light went on, the fan whirring softly into life. I stayed motionless. Depending on where the intruder was in the house when the light had gone out, he might think—assume—I had turned out the lamp and gone upstairs. Or maybe not.

He stood inside the doorway listening for me. I could feel him in the strained silence.

Except that it wasn't silent. Buck was barking hysterically, and then the barking cut off on a screech.

"Buck?" Stephen called from the front of the house.

And we were out of time. The footsteps started back down the hallway toward the front door. I scrambled up from behind the desk and followed him—a bulky figure in black wearing a dark ski mask. He was not fast on his feet. I caught him up in three steps. He spun around, and I slammed him over the head with the paperweight. He slumped to the floor, and I stepped over him and picked up his fallen pistol—a Heckler & Koch SOCOM specially fitted with a sound and flash suppressor. Fitted with an infrared laser sight as well, but the would-be assassin wasn't wearing goggles—which was the first good news I'd had in twenty-four hours.

A second man was coming through the back porch door. I shot him in the chest with the silenced gun and he fell back out the door, the porch door swinging back with a bang against the house. I turned out the kitchen light. Turned out the porch light as I reached the back door—just in time to see Stephen coming around the corner of the house.

"Get down!" I yelled, stepping over the dying man feebly waving a pistol my way. I kicked him hard in the head, plucking the pistol from his hand. Putting the safety on, I wedged it in my back waistband.

About half a second later a Micro Uzi raked the side of the house, stitching bullets through the walls and windows. Glass shattered, wood splintered from inside the house. I was already scrambling to the end of the porch, peering down through the railing.

"Stephen? Jesus. *Stephen*?"

To my relief he was crouched in the flowerbed. He looked up, unhurt, his face a pale glimmer.

I felt almost dizzy with relief. "Are you all right? You're not hurt?"

"What the fuck is this?" He sounded shaken but there was no panic in his voice. Anger, yes. Outrage. Fear. But all of it under control.

"It's another long story." I wished he wasn't wearing a white shirt.

"I heard Buck squeal," he said. "They shot him, didn't they?"

"I'm sorry."

"*Goddamn you,*" he said quietly and intensely, and I flinched.

There was another burst of machine gun fire. Bullets tore through the wood of the porch posts, the swing's canvas, hitting stone and wood and glass.

I whispered into the silence that followed, "I'll lay down a covering fire. If you could climb up here?"

He nodded curtly.

I slid across the wood flooring to one of the stone and wood pillars, stood—making myself as narrow a target as possible, and began methodically firing in the direction of the lake. I could hear the ducks and geese in a panic, saw them taking wing against the night sky.

Behind me I heard Stephen climb onto the porch.

The gunman by the lake answered back with bullets. They gouged the stone pillar in front of me, took chunks out of the wooden overhang. I watched for the muzzle flash, holding my fire.

Behind me Stephen was speaking rapidly in a low steady voice—though apparently not to me.

There was a pause in the festivities. I glanced around. He was on his cell phone calling for help. And I was proud of how cool he sounded. His father would have been proud too. And all those generations of Johnny Rebs.

He closed his cell phone. I squatted, offering him the pistol I'd taken off the second assassin, but he shook his head.

"For God's sake, Stephen. You've handled a gun before."

"I haven't shot a rifle in over a decade. And I sure as hell never shot at anything capable of firing back. I'd be worse than useless with that," he said.

I gnawed my lip, thinking. Maybe he was right. I said, "I'll cover you again. Get inside the house and barricade yourself in the cellar."

"What are you going to do?"

"What I'm trained to do."

"No." He was shaking his head. "Help is on the way. We just need to wait it out."

"That's exactly what we're going to do. Only I'm waiting out here. And you're waiting inside."

"I'm not hiding in the goddamn cellar while you're up here getting shot at!"

There was another short burst of machine gun fire. Stephen pressed down lower to the wooden planks. I ducked against the stone pillar. I thought the gunman was angling around for better position. Into the pause that followed, I said, "We don't have a lot of time to debate this."

He said furiously, "I'm not leaving you under fire!"

"Goddamn it. Do I tell you how to fix a broken leg? Do what I ask before you get us both killed."

He was shaking his head stubbornly, and I said desperately, "Please. All right? Stephen, *please* go to the fucking cellar so I can go after this son of a bitch without having to worry about you."

And to my bewilderment, he laughed, a breathless gust of sound and scooted over to the post where I crouched. "The magic word? Is that what you think I'm waiting for?" He grabbed me by my shoulders. "Listen to me. There's a magic word all right. It's love."

I gaped at him. "Stephen —"

"Listen to me."

I threw a look over my shoulder. Beyond the trees I could see the black glitter of the lake. The third gunman was out there somewhere, moving through the reeds, coming toward the house. And there might be more of them as well.

"Listen to me," Stephen repeated, and I switched my attention distractedly back to him. "I can't take it if something happens to you. I've spent the last two years living in fear every time the news reported a British citizen arrested for spying. Or a British soldier captured. Or killed."

"I'll be all right. And—anyway, there's nothing to blame yourself for. I brought this on."

His fingers dug in painfully. "No. You're not paying attention. I've spent the last four hours trying to convince Bryce—and myself—that I don't love you."

I admit that did get my attention. "Come again?"

He took my face in both his hands and kissed my mouth—and it was all there in that hard warm press of lips. I felt shaken as I pulled away.

"Don't throw your life away," Stephen said.

"I...don't intend to." I swallowed.

He stared at me, and I was almost grateful for the shadows that hid our expressions from each other. It went through my mind that he might be saying this—saying anything to keep me from further harm—but I dismissed the thought. This was Stephen and he wouldn't lie about this. Not even to keep me from throwing my life away.

"I won't let you down again," I said.

To my relief he nodded once, curtly, and turned away. I rose and began firing at the reeds moving in the distance. Stephen dashed for the door, jumping over the dead man, disappearing inside the darkened house.

The Heckler & Koch clicked on empty. I set it aside and pulled out the pistol I'd taken from the second assassin. A Beretta M92F. Fifteen rounds in the magazine, so I needed to make every shot count. I called softly, "Stephen?"

He answered from inside the kitchen, equally softly.

I said, "Watch yourself. There could be someone inside."

If he answered, I didn't hear it. I dropped down and scooted across the porch to the railing, letting myself over the side and landing on the grass in a crouch.

Silence. I could hear the weathervane high above moving rustily in the breeze. A rose trellis knocking against the side of the house. Down by the water, the ducks and geese were still having fits. Light shone from the front room, casting a yellow oblong across the grass and flowerbed.

As I watched, I saw the red fiber-optic beam of a laser slide along the front of the porch, probing the shadows—and I smiled. *I spy with my little eye...* Eleven to eighteen yards away. That put him on the edge of the reeds toward the west end of the house. Better yet, he believed I was somewhere on the porch.

I sprinted to the nearest magnolia, rested my spine against it.

The geese continued to cackle and honk near the water's edge. I looked back at the house. The living room light had gone out. The house appeared quiet and still. I turned my attention to the lake.

I wondered how long till we got reinforcements. Better—much better—if this ended here and now. Arrest meant a trial. Trial meant publicity. Publicity would be very bad news. For me. For Stephen.

I waited.

The red laser dot disappeared.

What now?

I darted to the next tree.

Nothing.

I slid down on my haunches, back against the trunk, waiting. The stitches in my thigh throbbed in time to my heartbeat. The good old femoral artery pulsing away next to all those careful little stitches. My ribs ached as I tried to draw a deep breath. I wiped my forehead. Waited.

Just as the would-be assassin appeared to be doing.

I risked another look around the tree trunk. I could see the pinpoints of starlight like tiny candles drifting on the water, and strangely a line from *Little Dorrit* came into my mind: *While the flowers, pale and unreal in the moonlight, floated away upon the river; and thus do greater things that once were in our breasts, and near our hearts, flow from us to the eternal seas.*

I could taste Stephen's kiss on my lips. Somewhere to my left I could hear a funny, low whining. My eyes raked the darkness, picking out a long black shadow within the other shadows. Buck. He lay in the deep grass beneath the tall trees.

I considered him. "Lie still, Buck," I said keeping my voice low.

He whined and lifted his head a little.

Bullets thunked into wood above my head as the Uzi opened up again. I yelled like I'd been hit, threw myself in the grass, flat as I could get, head raised just enough to see over my hands as I steadied the Beretta.

Such an old trick. But then one reason it had been around forever was because it worked so well. He stood up out of the reeds, machine gun at ready, striding up the embankment toward where I lay motionless.

I took careful sight. The light was poor and my hands were not quite steady. I had to wait longer than I wanted to be sure I had him. I fired. The bullet hit him low in his left shoulder. He screamed and fired. Grass chewed up next to me in great gobs of mud and green. I rolled away and fired again, this time hitting him dead center.

He went down, firing, bullets plowing into the ground until he slumped forward.

For a time I lay there panting, heart hammering, watching him. He didn't move.

I got up, bracing myself with my free hand, walked over to him, pistol trained. I planted one foot on the machine gun barrel, rolled him over with my other. His eyes stared frozenly through the holes in the ski mask.

Kneeling, I felt him over quickly, took a pistol off him, pulled the machine gun out of his hand, and walked back up the slope. I stopped beside Buck, knelt painfully. He whined again, thumped his tail feebly.

"Good dog," I muttered. His fur was sticky with blood, but the bullet had taken him in the shoulder. I stroked his coat. Considered trying to carry him, but there was no way with my ribs, and dropping him was not going to be beneficial.

"Stay, Buck," I ordered, as he thrashed around, trying to get up. He subsided, whining. I gave him a final pat and rose.

The house stood dark and silent as I approached. I brought the pistol up, moving quietly onto the porch. The dead assassin sprawled in the doorway. I stepped over him, moved across the kitchen, picking my way through glass and pottery, pulped fruit, and splintered wood.

The fridge was silent, mortally wounded. The clock ticked peacefully on the wall. The door leading down to the cellar was closed.

I moved into the hall. The lack of light made it nearly impossible to see. I moved forward silently.

Moonlight spilled onto the floorboards outside the study door. The first assassin was gone.

Jesus fucking Christ. That was my fault for not wanting to soak Stephen's floorboards with blood. I prayed my carelessness hadn't resulted in harm —

Harm. I couldn't consider anything beyond that.

Maybe the assassin had fled when he regained consciousness.

Maybe Stephen had hauled him downstairs to his office to patch him up. Just like Stephen, that.

Or maybe he had taken Stephen hostage.

Maybe he'd slit his throat.

My stomach roiled in sick panic. *Shut it,* I thought fiercely.

I stepped back into the kitchen, finding my way through the utility room with the washer and dryer to the cellar door. It swung open silently.

Flattening myself against the wall, I whispered, "Stephen?"

Nothing.

It was a struggle to control my growing dread. I couldn't think beyond the fact that Stephen might already be dead and it was my fault.

I felt for the wall switch, found it. Light flared on illuminating the cellar. Wine racks neatly lined one side, and on the other, shelves with canned goods, bottled water, tins, Christmas decorations. No sign of Stephen—but no sign of violence either.

Then something hit me from behind and I went crashing down the staircase with someone on top of me.

I landed at the bottom, half-stunned, my crushed ribs screaming protest. Wriggling, I tried to get out from under the weight pinning me to the floor. My right shoulder felt dislocated, and I felt frantically with my left hand for the pistol I'd dropped.

Hands locked around my throat. I stared up into black eyes behind a glistening, blood-soaked ski mask. The weight on my damaged ribs was red agony, making it difficult to think and nearly impossible to breathe. I grabbed for his hands, trying to secure one of his arms, but my right arm still wasn't cooperating. I threw my foot over his same side foot—and tried to buck him off.

He nearly toppled, but managed to keep his hold on my throat, sinking his fingers in deeper, and I wheezed for breath. One-handed, I couldn't break his grip and I was beginning to see stars shooting through the red tide.

Stone fragments stung my face. The rifle shot was deafening, echoing around the stone walls as the bullet plowed into the cement floor next to me. The hands around my throat stiffened—then loosened. Blood spilled out of the hole in my attacker's chest. He pitched forward, landing half on top of me, half beside me.

I gulped for air, dragging sweet oxygen into my laboring lungs, and the dark receded from the edges of my vision.

Staring past the meaty shoulder pressing into me, I saw Stephen coming down the cellar stairs fast, rifle in hand. I wanted to tell him to be careful, to take no chances, but my bruised throat wouldn't work.

He rolled my attacker off me.

"Were you hit? I had to take the shot. I was afraid he'd break your neck." He was talking to me, but his voice sounded odd and his face was the face of a stranger as he knelt and checked the man he'd shot.

Checked to see if he was alive. If he could be saved. Because that's what Stephen did. Healed people. Saved lives.

Until tonight.

I tried to push up, and the pain nearly blacked me out again. He laid the rifle down, turning to me. "Don't try to move. Just tell me where you're hurt."

I shook my head, reaching for him—needing to see, verify by touch, that he was really all right, really unhurt. I'd been so sure he was dead. That I'd caused his death.

He was shaking as he took me into his arms but his hands were gentle and professional as he felt me over, checking for injuries.

I croaked, "I'm all right. Are you sure you're not…?" I saw his face then. Saw beyond the quiet control. Saw the shock and the horror. Saw the depth of heartsickness in his eyes and understood a little of what this blooding had cost him. What *I* had cost him. And finally, too late, I grasped how deluded I'd been, convincing myself that coming back was the way to make everything right, was the best thing for all concerned. Arrogant and stupid and selfish from start to finish. What the hell was there left to say? *Sorry? Forgive me?* Requiring more from him, this time his absolution for my own sins.

"What is it?" he said, alarmed. "Mark?"

I managed to get my battered vocal cords to cooperate. "Thank you…for…"

For my life.

His face twisted. "I'd never let anyone hurt you, you know that," he said.

I lost it. Suddenly I was sobbing. I couldn't stop.

Quite calmly, he gathered me to him, and astonishingly what he said was, "That's right. Let go. Let it out. That's just what you need."

It was the last thing on earth I needed. I shook my head but the tears wouldn't stop.

And Stephen held me through it all, as though this were perfectly normal behavior, nothing to be ashamed of. In my whole life no one ever gave me permission to fall apart, to let go. He was the only person in the world who thought I needed taking care of, protecting.

"Is any of this blood yours?" he asked, his hand moving carefully over my gore-soaked shirt.

I pulled back a little. Wiped my face with my hand, then my sleeve. My eyes were still leaking, but the worst was over. "Literally or metaphorically?" I got out.

"What kind of talk is that?" he muttered, pulling me against him, and he kissed my wet eyes.

It was…something inside me melted away, and I leaned against him. I said helplessly, "I thought you were dead. That I'd killed you. I shouldn't have come back. I knew it but I —"

"Stop it." His vehemence stopped me. "Don't say that again."

I nodded, wiped my face in his shirt. It was embarrassing to have fallen apart with him like that, and yet…it was liberating. Cleansing.

"Can you stand?"

I nodded tiredly, sat up. Remembered something, clutching at him with my good hand. "Buck! He's not dead. At least he wasn't fifteen minutes ago."

"Okay. Let's get you on your feet. Hold your right arm against your chest."

I obeyed. He hooked an arm around my waist and lifted me to my feet, and I managed not to throw up or black out. He walked me over the dead terrorist, and then got me up the stairs. As we reached the kitchen I heard the sound of sirens in the distance.

That reminded me that I had phone calls to make as well. My brain just didn't seem to be working. I wiped a hand across my wet lashes.

"Go get Buck," I said, pulling away. "I can handle this."

* * * * *

The mattress dipped. I came to groggily, lifting my head. In the dawn's early light, I could see Stephen climbing into bed beside me.

"It's just me," he said.

Which somehow seemed like the understatement of the year. We had only finished talking with law enforcement an hour or so earlier. Stephen had finished patching up the wounded—me—and the bodies had been carted away.

"How's Buck?" I asked. My voice was raspy from the bruising on my throat.

I had crashed not long after the vet had arrived. Stephen said, "I think he's going to be all right. John's hopeful that because of his age and his general condition, he'll pull through."

"That's good."

"How are you?" He stretched out beside me, and I moved awkwardly into his arms. He hugged me, careful of my shoulder—and ribs—and leg.

"I'm all right." And I realized I was. I studied his drawn face. "How are you?"

He met my eyes. "I'll be all right."

I swallowed over the blockage in my throat. "I'm sorry, Stephen. I can't tell you how sorry."

"I know. And you've got plenty to be sorry for." His smile was faint. "But not that. You're lying here next to me, alive, and that makes all the difference in the world."

My eyes prickled again, and I closed them. I couldn't remember crying since I was a little kid, but apparently I was making up for lost time.

He said gently, "If those tears are for me, they're not necessary."

I nodded. Took a deep breath and managed to get control. I opened my eyes again. "What changed?" I asked. "Last night you sounded pretty sure it was over."

"Then you're the one person I managed to convince." He nuzzled my face, finding my mouth with his—about the only part of my body that didn't hurt. I put my good arm around him, ignoring the pain of my ribs. He kissed me softly, mouth, nose, eyes.

He said, "I guess I finally faced the fact that by sending you away I was just hurrying up the thing I was afraid of all along."

"I know what I want now. And I won't leave you ever again."

He smiled, not entirely convinced. It didn't matter because I knew I was telling the truth, and convincing him in the days to come would be its own reward.

He asked at last, "Can you tell me now what happened to you?"

I lay quietly, watching his face. "I've told you most of it." Dawn cast an uncertain watery light, like the tints in Dulac's illustrations of the *Rubaiyat*. Stephen's eyes looked gray and unreadable. I said, "I was in Kandahar with another agent."

"Barry," he said.

"Barry Shelton, yes." I closed my eyes. It was easier like that. "Taliban resistance is very strong in that part of the country. Ostensibly we were there on a fact-finding mission, but we were actually there to shore up wavering support from local tribes for the US and UK efforts."

He brushed the knuckles of his hand against the lower part of my jaw—where the skin was paler from the beard I had worn for months. "Go on."

I opened my eyes. I found I wanted to watch his face, after all. "We were sold out. Betrayed. I don't know by whom. Or why. It doesn't matter. It's nothing new. Nothing that hasn't happened before. Nothing that won't happen again. To someone else."

"What happened?"

"We went to meet with a local warlord, and we were taken prisoner." I swallowed, seeing it all again, feeling the fists, the boots, seeing the naked hate in the faces that had smiled a few minutes before. Reliving the sick helplessness, the brutal buzz of fear, knowing what was ahead for us. "They were transporting us across the border. Our allies attacked. Created enough of a diversion that we were able to get free. I managed to escape. Barry was killed. Shot."

"And you decided you'd finally had enough."

It was important that he understand this. I said, "I'd decided I'd had enough before I ever went. The last time we talked...when you said it was over—I decided then that if, *when*, I got home—I was packing it in. That if you'd have me, I'd try and make it up to you. I know you don't believe that."

He interrupted. "I was angry and disappointed. I thought for my own sake, I needed to move on. We'd lost two years together, and I didn't know if you'd ever see your way to settling down. I thought you'd changed your mind—and I didn't blame you because, frankly, about the most excitement we see around here is when Buck corners a possum."

"I suppose it depends on your definition of excitement. Personally..."

He said, "I'm not saying it doesn't have its moments."

He tried to be careful with me, but as much as I craved his tenderness, I needed something more, needed to reassure myself that he was really mine, that it wasn't just kindness or self-sacrifice. He took it with bemused, heavy-lidded calm, kissing my face, my bruised throat as I clutched him, nuzzled his hair and thrust awkwardly into his taut, aroused body.

"Easy, easy. You're going to break something," he murmured, his mouth finding my lips. He rubbed his cheek against mine, his beard rasping teasingly against my sensitized skin.

"Sorry." I tried to slow myself down, catching my breath in pained little gulps. "Am I hurting you?" It felt so good sheathed deep inside his body, the dark velvet grip that owned me even as I tried to possess him. I stilled my movements with an effort.

"Not me." His hands slid down my sides, trying to ease my position. "You." His hands settled on my arse, stroking with feathering fingertips.

And I chuckled, surprising him, because broken bones notwithstanding, for the first time in my life I felt completely whole.

* * * * *

"Now what in the world is that?" remarked Lena, staring out the window over the sink as we had breakfast in the kitchen alcove the following day. "As if we haven't had enough trouble around here."

"Well, what do you know," Stephen said grimly. "I think the mountain has decided it would be faster to visit Mohammed."

I looked up sharply from my blueberry French toast in time to watch a helicopter rocking slowly down behind the trees to settle by the lake.

The geese, who had finally returned after the excitement of thirty-six hours earlier, took flight once more. The reeds around the lake whipped in the wind from the helicopter blades.

"Goddamn it," I said, and Lena made a disapproving noise.

As we stared, the door to the helicopter opened and a young man hopped out. He turned to help a tall and familiar figure disembark. Even from where we sat I recognized the shock of white hair and stooped shoulders. "It's the Old Man himself," I said in disbelief.

Stephen swore quietly.

I rose and went out onto the porch. Stephen followed me down the hill, past the yellow crime scene tape marking off the gun battle of two nights earlier.

The old man, impeccably tailored as always, strode toward us, moving with that characteristic decisiveness and dispatch. He held an official-looking manila envelop.

“Well, Mr. Hardwicke,” he said as he reached us, his eyes taking in Stephen standing calmly at my shoulder. “It’s nice to see you looking so well. I was led to believe your health was in a far more precarious state.”

“Just seeing you again is a tonic, sir,” I said gravely.

The wind whipped his long white hair over his forehead and he raked it back impatiently, glaring at us with his pale blue eyes. Then his shoulders slumped and he sighed. “I shall miss you, Mark. I had you earmarked for bigger and better things. However, ours is an organization that does not thrive in the limelight, and events of the past few days have brought undue and unwelcome attention your way—and thus our way.”

He handed me the envelope.

Stephen snorted. “You’re giving him his pink slip?”

The Old Man said haughtily, “I think Mr. Hardwicke will agree the terms are quite generous—provided he agrees to all our terms.”

“Terms?” Stephen inquired warily, looking from me to my employer. “What are we talking about here? A no compete?”

I felt my mouth twitching into an inappropriate smile, but catching the Old Man’s glare, I bit it back. “I have to agree to keep my mouth shut.” As Stephen’s eyes narrowed, I added, “I hope I can find work teaching because I won’t be able to write that bestselling roman à clef after all.”

“You won’t starve,” the Old Man said.

“Thank you, sir,” I said, and I meant it. I didn’t care about my pension. He was letting me go without a fuss, and that was all that mattered to me now.

The Old Man nodded curtly, and started to turn away. I realized that I would probably never see him again.

I said, “Sir, would you care for some breakfast before you head back?” Stephen threw me a look of disbelief.

The Old Man fastened that pale gaze on me. “No, thank you, Mr. Hardwicke. I must be away. I merely happened to be in the neighborhood.”

“Ah.”

He turned, then paused. “There is one final thing. You may hear on the news tonight that several high ranking Taliban were killed in a missile attack in Kandahar yesterday. One of the dead has been confirmed as Mullah Arsullah.”

I stared at him. It seemed too much to hope for, but I couldn’t see any point in his lying about it.

“There’s no mistake?”

“There’s no mistake.” Just for an instant there was something I had rarely seen in his eyes—something I’d used to crave—an emotion dangerously akin to affection. “Let us hope, Mr. Hardwicke, that you don’t grow bored with what seems destined to be a very long and uneventful retirement.”

“Not much chance of that, sir.”

In silence we watched as he made his way swiftly down the hill, climbed back into the helicopter. The blades picked up speed, the helicopter lifted and whirled away. In a few moments it was a tiny speck in the distance.

Stephen's hand rested warmly on my shoulder, and I turned to him.

"Welcome home," he said.

I Spy Something Wicked

Josh Lanyon

Chapter One

The Glock was taped beneath my seat. I freed it, reached for the magazine in the glove compartment, and palmed it into the frame. I scanned the empty car park, the black windows of the house in front of me.

I spy with my little eye…

Nothing moved. The bronze autumn moon shone brightly through the barren branches crosshatching the bell-cast rooftops.

I turned off the radio in the dashboard console, cutting off Jack White midnote. "Dead leaves and dirty ground" was about right. I unlocked the door of the Range Rover, got out, and crossed the deserted lot, boots crunching on gravel, breath hanging in the chilly October night. There was a hint of wood smoke in the air; the nearest house was roughly eight kilometers away. A full five miles to the nearest living soul.

I walked past a large banner sign lying facedown in the frosty grass and studied the building's facade. Two stories of battered white stone. Broken finials and dentils. Arched windows — broken on the top level, mostly boarded on the bottom. The narrow, arched front door was also boarded up. Once upon a time, this had been some founding family's mansion; in the early part of the last century, it had operated as a funhouse. Now it looked like a haunted house. That was appropriate since I was there to meet a ghost.

I went around to the side of the long building, found a window where the boarding had been ripped away. I hoisted myself up and scrambled over the sill.

Inside, moonlight highlighted a checkerboard floor and what appeared to be broken sections of an enormous wooden slide.

According to Stephen, it was a long time, decades, since the place had operated officially, but it was a popular place for teens to romance — and vandalize. Especially around Halloween. That was two nights away. I didn't anticipate any interruptions.

I proceeded, soft-footed, along an accordion strip of mirrors, some broken, some not, my reflection flashing past: a man of medium height, thin, dark, nondescript. The pistol gleamed in my hand like a star.

Down a short flight of stairs, a twist and a turn, another short flight down. I froze. At the bottom of the steps, a woman sat hunched over. She wore tattered French knickers and a blonde wig. It took a couple of seconds to realize she was covered in cobwebs. One of those mechanical mannequins. I glanced at her in passing and saw that someone had bashed her face in.

A floorboard squeaked. I spun, bringing the pistol up. Jesus. He'd arrived before me. I was getting sloppy in my old age.

The shadow raised its arms high. Hands empty.

"Christ on a crutch, Hardwicke. I don't think much of your taste in meeting places."

I lowered my pistol. "Malik."

He continued to bitch. "Really, old boy. Don't see why we couldn't have done this in more comfortable surroundings. Some place civilized where we might have a drink and a chat."

Why? Because I thought I might have to kill him. But I wasn't so socially inept as to say that — for all Stephen thinks, I'm lacking in the social graces. Instead, I replied, "I like my privacy."

"So I gathered. May I put my hands down?"

"Yes. But keep them where I can see them."

He suddenly laughed. "Christ on a crutch! You think I'm here to twep you!"

"Good luck with that."

He was still chuckling; I didn't find it nearly as amusing. "You think the Old Man ordered an executive action against you?"

"How should I know?"

"Just the opposite, mate. He needs your help."

I relaxed a fraction. "Sorry. I'm no longer in the help business."

"Private citizen, eh? How's that going for you? I should think you'd be climbing the walls with boredom by now."

"You don't know me."

"Course I do. You're just like me. Like all of us in The Section."

"I'm not in The Section. I'm retired. Happily retired."

"So we heard. Decided to get married and grow roses. Think I'd prefer Oppenheim Memorial Park. You know, the lads have a bit of a wager going on how long you'll last in the private sector. Granted, you've lasted four months longer than I thought you would. Tigers don't change their spots."

I didn't bother to correct him. Not about the spotty tigers, and not about the fact that I was quite content in my role as private citizen.

Mostly. According to Stephen, I still had a lot to learn about "coloring between the lines."

Malik was saying, "You must have seen the news. You must know what's going on in Afghanistan with Operation Herrick."

"I watched the UK death toll pass two hundred."

"That, yes. But I mean what's happening with the Old Man. The heat he's taking from the cabinet and the ministers."

"Nothing he hasn't faced before."

"It's different this time."

If I had tuppence for every time I've heard that.

"No." I was already turning away. "I can't help." This was a promise I wasn't going to break. Not for anyone. Not even John Holohan.

Malik cried, "Hear me out at least, can't you?"

His vehemence surprised me. I faced him, saying nothing. I didn't want to hear it. Wasn't going to let it change anything. But…I owed John this much; I'd hear his emissary out.

Malik said, "He's fighting for his survival."

Welcome to the club, I thought. I didn't say it.

Malik was Anglo-Indian, a few years younger than I was, and quite good-looking. Medium height, slim and dark; just the way John liked 'em. I should know. He was saying earnestly, "You know what the political climate is like these days. What the media are like. They're making him the scapegoat for two decades' worth of gutless policy and bad decisions. They're trying to make him pay for policies he fought tooth and nail to prevent."

I did know. But ever the hard man, I said, "Everyone has to pack it in sooner or later. Even the Old Man. Did he think they were going to let him run forever? He must be near the mandatory age of retirement as it is."

"We're not discussing retirement. We're talking about disgrace, scandal, the ruin of a brilliant career. Is that what you want for him?"

I had no answer. I didn't want that for John. He didn't deserve that. But I had given my word to Stephen. And I was never going to disappoint Stephen again. Never give him grounds to regret giving me that second chance.

"If you do this for him, he'll never bother you again."

I nearly laughed — although it wasn't funny. "Do you know how many times I've heard that?"

"Look, Hardwicke, it's the world we live in. Promises…well, there are no guarantees in this life. If anyone should know that, you should."

"You're not helping your case."

"He wouldn't ask if there was another way."

"Right, well speaking of that, why didn't he come himself then? Why'd he send you?"

"They're watching him. The media. The other agencies. He can't step outside his door without someone from the press trying to snap his picture. It's chaos. We can't operate like that. The Section requires secrecy to remain effective."

I could not afford to care about this. To even ask the question aloud was an indicator to both of us, but I heard my voice, reluctance evident. "What does he want me to do?"

"He wants you to go back to Afghanistan. Use your influence with Pashtun tribal leaders in Helmand to back our play. To support British and NATO forces against the Taliban in Operation Sword Strike."

"I can't go back there!" Whatever I'd expected to hear, it wasn't this. Maybe it was naïve, but I was genuinely shocked. No one knew better than John Holohan why I couldn't ever return to that region.

"You've got the friends; you've got the network."

"My contacts are dead. My network was blown with me. There's a price on my head."

"No one's asking you to stay in. It's just a-a cakewalk COA. Touch base and config alliances for the big push, then bombshell out."

I'd forgotten how much I hated the self-important acronyms and slang. I stared at his fierce face, and suddenly it all made sense.

"Jesus. You're in love with him. You're in love with John."

"What of it?" I could see him bristling. "Not the first, am I?"

No. Not by a long shot. Nor the last, though I didn't tell him so. I said, "Your opinion on this is not exactly objective."

His Adam's apple jumped in the wavering light. "No, I'm not objective. Neither should you be. Not with what you owe him."

"I don't owe him fuck."

Malik's mouth curled into a semblance of a smile. "You wouldn't be angry if you didn't believe it was true. Listen, you know — we all know — he let you walk away unscathed. He didn't have to do that. He even saw to it you got your full bloody pension."

I was shaking my head, refusing this, refusing what he was asking. My death. That's what he was asking.

"No one else can do this," he insisted fiercely.

"Then it won't be done."

"You ungrateful, sodding bastard. And he holds *you* up as the paragon of loyalty!"

"Go to hell."

That was my cue. My exit line.

I didn't move.

And as the seconds passed, and as we stood there, furious, breathing hard, glaring at each other, I saw Malik's face change. Saw him recognize that I had not turned and walked away when I should have.

That I was considering it.

I said slowly, unwillingly, "When do you need an answer?"

"I can give you forty-eight hours."

I clenched my jaw on the things I wanted to say. I needed to think. Think hard. As much as I wanted to refuse — I wasn't sure I could. I said at last, bitterly, "You'll have my answer in forty-eight hours."

I let Malik leave first. Waited with the faded clowns and broken toys for his footsteps to die away, listened for the faraway growl of his motorbike to be swallowed by the hungry autumn night.

Silence settled. Sank its claws in.

I couldn't go home yet. Couldn't face Stephen. Not till I'd figured out what to tell him. What was it Dickens said? *An idea, like a ghost, must be spoken to a little before it will explain itself.*

A shadowrun. A black op. That was what the Old Man was asking. Sending me in as an illegal, naked into hostile territory. Knowing I was blown, knowing there was a price on my head, he was asking me to go back. Yes, that would take a little explaining. To Stephen — and to myself.

When I decided it was clear, I headed back to where I'd parked. The Range Rover's headlamps blinked as I pressed the key fob. In that flash of light I saw a shadow detach itself from the trees and glide toward me. I laced the Rover's keys between my fingers like makeshift brass knuckles, and when he grabbed me, I went with the momentum, using it against him, flipping him over. He landed on his back in the dead leaves, his breath expelling in a hard *oof.*

I knelt on his scrawny chest using my left foot to grind his flailing right hand into the ground, my right pinning his left wrist. With my free hand I pressed the point of the longest blade in my key ring against his carotid artery.

"Surprise, surprise," I said gently, and pressed a little harder just to make my…point.

He wheezed in panic, his eyes bulging. Clearly an amateur. I studied him in the colorless moonlight. Narrow nose; close-set brown eyes; a small mouth; lank, greasy dark hair. An unlovely specimen. I didn't know him.

He blubbered something lost in spit and snot.

"Didn't catch that," I said. And then, "Don't move if you don't want an emergency tracheotomy."

He held still — if we didn't count the trembling — and I felt around, found his wallet, flipped it open, and checked his driver's ID.

Bradley Kaine.

It meant nothing to me. Age 31. No occupation, but I'd already guessed it: loser.

I made a mental note of his address.

"I'm trying to think of a good reason not to punch a hole in your throat, Bradley. Nothing occurs to me."

More inarticulate protests.

"What were you doing here? Planning a spot of B and E? Nah. Nothing worth stealing in there. Waiting for some poor old wino to roll? No. Winos are in short supply here. Waiting to rob some kid and his bird? Hmm? That's it, I bet. A spot of robbery and rape?"

He frantically shook his head.

"Course you were. Nothing personal, right? It's what you do. What you are." The temptation was to kill him, this miserable scrap of an excuse for a man, this predator who waited in the shadows for someone smaller, younger, weaker.

Someone like me — but without my peculiar brand of skills.

I said harshly, "You weren't out here stargazing, we both know that."

He gibbered something, little flecks of spittle hitting my face.

He was revolting. The perfect companion for an already bad day. I clenched my keys so hard, my hand shook, denting his clammy flesh. It was all I could do to control the disquieting urge to give release to the rage and frustration churning inside me.

He began to cry. The pungent stink of ammonia reached my nostrils. In his terror he'd pissed himself.

"Shut it," I bit out. "I'm going to let you live. I'm going to give you a second chance. If I ever see you here again, I will kill you. Got it?"

He nodded feverishly.

I took my keys out of his throat, eased my boot off his hand, stood, and stepped back. He continued to lie on the ground, sobbing.

Pitiable. But I felt no pity. Something terrible had had happened to me over the years, had killed something inside me. Were I Stephen, I would feel compassion for him. I would hope that this was a turning point in his life. But being me, I only thought that it was probably a mistake to let him go. Even if it was dark enough to obscure my features, not so many blokes with English accents hanging about. I felt no compassion. I was letting him live because I knew that was what Stephen would do.

* * * * *

I parked in the tree-lined circular drive of the white Victorian mansion. The lights were on downstairs, the curtains wide open. It was like looking into a doll house or a stage set. Downstairs I could see Buck curled up on the sofa in the den. The bookshelves where my books now crowded Stephen's. My paintings symmetrically arranged around Stephen's. Upstairs, Stephen walked from the bathroom into the bedroom. He wore a pair of pale green pajama bottoms. He was toweling his hair.

I sighed. Despite my best efforts, I couldn't get Stephen to take the concept of security seriously. Granted, he was better than he had been; he remembered to lock the doors now, at least. But that was just to relieve my mind. When I'd tried to explain why this was so important, bewilderingly, he'd apologized and said, "I know you need to feel secure. I promise to be more careful." As though it were about *my* safety. About my *feelings*.

I ejected the magazine from the Glock and dropped it back into the glove compartment. I bent, re-taped the pistol beneath the seat, got out of the Range Rover, locked it, and went quickly up the stone steps to the long, covered porch. There was a pyramid of resin jack-o-lanterns at the base of one of the posts, electric eyes and smiles glowing brightly. Black rubber bats on string hung from the porch rafters, stirring in the breeze.

As I locked the front door behind me, Buck came to greet me, tail wagging while he growled in that way of Chesapeake Bay retrievers. He'd been shot back in May when a team of assassins hired by a senior Taliban commander had come calling for me, but he was doing fine now. A little stiff in the mornings, but — as Stephen had gently teased — who wasn't?

Upstairs, the stereo was playing. I could hear the music drifting down the staircase: simple, intensely emotional, and somehow fragile. Barber's *Adagio for Strings*. An appropriate soundtrack for the return of old ghosts.

Trailed by Buck, I went around checking windows and closing curtains. I was relieved to see that while Stephen hadn't bothered with the curtains, he had at least locked everything.

In the kitchen, I poured myself a glass of milk and leaned against the sink while staring out at the black diamond glitter of the lake behind the house. I hadn't been able to spare time for dinner, but I wasn't hungry. It had been a long day. I was taking courses at the University of Shenandoah, their Career Switcher Program, which was designed for people like me, frustrated teachers who hadn't completed the training curriculum but had "considerable life experiences, career achievements, and academic backgrounds that are relevant."

Apparently I'd have been better off reporting to the target range every day and practicing my Pashto. In the mountains of Afghanistan they have a saying: *A wolf cannot outrun its shadow.*

I tried again to think how I would tell Stephen, how I would explain what I was considering, and I decided that it would be better to work it out in my mind first. I was too angry and confused just now — and Stephen had zero tolerance for the Old Man even at the best of times.

I washed the glass, rinsed it, and set in the sink. I turned out the lights and went upstairs.

Stephen was in bed, reading the *New England Journal of Medicine*.

He glanced up, and smiled, and my heart did that little flip it always did. He was so…beautiful. At fifty he made everyone else look callow and crude. Tall, lean, broad shoulders and long legs. His hair was prematurely silver, but it just emphasized how young and handsome he really was. He looked like the quintessential doctor on the telly, a man you wouldn't think twice about trusting with your life or your heart.

I went to him and he kissed me, but as our lips parted, his green eyes were searching. He said, "You're late."

"Yes. Sorry."

He was waiting for an explanation. That was one of the difficult things about being with someone. Accountability. I just wasn't ready to discuss Malik's proposition with him, and I didn't want to lie, so I said nothing.

When I didn't offer an explanation, Stephen, patiently explaining the customs to a foreigner, said, "You should have phoned. I was worried."

"I wasn't thinking of that."

His mouth quirked wryly. "Obviously not." He was studying me, looking for clues. "Have you eaten?"

I shook my head. "Not hungry, really." I added quickly, as his brows drew together, "Not for food."

I loved the way the concern in his face gave way to that wicked grin. He tossed aside the journal and, reaching for me, murmured, "Oh yeah?"

I mimicked that soft Southern accent, "Oh *yeah*."

In the soft autumn darkness we came together, arms sliding around each other, holding each other close, entwined. The ghostly music tailed off, and there was nothing to hear but the slide and rustle of sheets and our rough breathing.

"I need you," I said. "I need you so much."

"You just take what you need," he urged me in that sexy whisper.

Always generous, though he insisted it was not generosity to give me what he wanted for himself. I tried to go slow, tried to be generous too, but I was tense and unhappy and a little frantic. I was rushing even as he tried to gentle me, kissing and caressing; I sped through the mechanics of preparation. There was almond oil in the bedside table. I uncapped it and slicked it over my cock, and then more slowly, tantalizingly over the thick length of Stephen's. Touching him like this, having the right to this intimacy was a joy in itself, and watching him writhe languidly against the sheets…was so beautiful. Sometimes he took the little bottle from me and insisted on petting and pampering me too, but tonight he simply submitted, and I was soothed by his acquiescence.

I fought the longing to give in to simple lust and just take him without more preliminary than that. Stephen was bigger than me, maybe even stronger than me, so there was something unstinting, even tender in this deliberate surrender to my own hunger. I trailed my mouth down his heaving chest; I rubbed my face against the silky, pale hair. I used my tongue to probe his navel, and Stephen squirmed sensuously, offering a husky chuckle.

Sometimes we made the foreplay last and last, but tonight I was too wound up and needy. After a very few minutes, I urged him onto his knees and guided the head of my cock into the black velvet heat of his body. Stephen cried out sweetly as I as impaled him, and then we were moving together. That feeling of being one, of union, of being so deep inside Stephen that I was part of him…I craved that as much as the physical release. But the physical release was exquisite.

Sometimes it scared me how good it was between us. What had I done to deserve it? Nothing. Not a damn thing.

Stephen's hips rose and shoved back, allowing me to thrust more deeply. It was frenetic and fierce — and way too fast. His uninhibited moans gave way to a sharp, sobbing cry as I emptied myself in pulses of warm salty fluid. Trembling, slick with sweat and other, it was all I could do not to crash down on him and knock him flat to the mattress. It didn't matter; he rolled over and with urgent hands pulled me up against his warm, powerful body.

"Sorry. Did you come?" I mumbled, guiltily, stroking his hip, seeking evidence.

"What do you think?" He was quietly amused.

We kissed and cuddled for the brief minutes before Stephen dropped off. I drowsed for a while, head on his chest, soothed by the sound of his heart beneath my ear.

And then I remembered Malik and all hope of sleep fled.

I began to go over our meeting again.

How could the Old Man ask this of me? He knew better than anyone —

It was very simple. I was going to refuse. I had to. I had given my word to Stephen. If I ever let him down again, it wouldn't matter if I survived Afghanistan or not. There wouldn't be a place for me in Stephen's home or heart.

I listened to the peaceful tenor of his breathing.

Carefully I slipped out of his arms. I inched open the bedside cabinet drawer, pulled out the pistol I kept there, and went downstairs.

At the kitchen table I spread out the things I needed to clean the G18. Not that it needed it. Glocks can shoot extreme amounts of ammo before cleaning is required, and I hadn't fired this one since I'd been to the target range the previous month. But I found the takedown and cleaning soothing, my hands moving automatically as I field stripped the pistol.

I racked the slide a couple of times. There was no round in the chamber; the magazine was upstairs in the drawer, but that's not the kind of thing you ever want to be get careless about. I aimed at the window over the sink and pulled the trigger to release the firing pin.

"What are you doing?" Stephen asked from behind me, and I nearly knocked the table over.

How the hell was I supposed to survive in the field when these days I wasn't even aware of someone coming up behind me in my own home?

I don't think I concealed my start from him, but I managed to drop back in the chair and say calmly, "Did I wake you? Sorry. I couldn't sleep."

"So you're cleaning your pistol?"

I shrugged. "It relaxes me."

He pulled the chair to the side of me out and sat down at the table, studying me. His eyebrows made a silver line of disapproval.

I grasped the slide, pulled it back, and pulled the release tabs.

I said, "It really only needs minimal lubrication for proper function. The main thing is to avoid getting oil or solvent into the striker channel."

"I'll keep that in mind."

I could feel him watching me.

"Is everything all right?" he asked finally.

I met his eyes briefly. Nodded.

"For a spy, you're not a very good liar."

"Ex-spy." Neither of us smiled. I said, "I can't lie to you. I don't want to try."

He eyes darkened. "What's going on, Mark? I thought when you got home you seemed strung up."

I shook my head. "I have to work some things out in my own mind before I try talking to you."

He said dryly, "Is it that hard to talk to me?"

"No, of course not." I put the gun down, but my hands were oily, so I ended up spreading them, palms up. "I…I'm just used to…keeping my own counsel."

"I know. That's not exactly what being in a relationship is about." He was giving me a long, narrow look — a look I hadn't seen since I'd returned bloodied and battered from Afghanistan the last time. "All right. I'm not going to try to winkle it out of you."

His chair scraped back. I looked up quickly. Stephen didn't appear angry, just tired.

"Let me know when you're ready to talk."

"I will. I promise." He turned away, and I said, "Stephen, it's nothing to do with us."

"Oh, for God's sake, Mark," he said disgustedly. He didn't bother to glance around as he left the room.

But when I crawled into bed two hours later, he sleepily welcomed me into his arms.

Funny thing, that, because I had never liked being held when I slept, but with Stephen there was something comforting about curling up against him. I liked his arms wrapped around me, liked the heat of him all down my back, the warm breath stirring the hair at the nape of my neck.

I loved him. That made all the difference.

Chapter Two

When I opened my eyes the next morning, it took me a few seconds to place myself after the violent chaos of my dreams. Uppermost was relief to realize that the nightmares had been just that, that the dangerous labyrinths I'd been wandering were imaginary. Then I remembered Malik, and my body seemed to freeze.

I turned my head, but I knew Stephen was already up; I could hear him humming in the shower. But I continued to stare at the indentation his head had made in the pillow next to mine. The sheets where he'd lain were warm, and when I hauled his pillow over to me, it carried his scent. I pressed it close to my face and breathed in deeply.

Picturing Stephen walking in and seeing me, I gave a shaky laugh and shoved the pillows and blankets aside.

The bathroom was warm and steamy and scented of something pleasantly herbal. It used to surprise me that Stephen went in for all these posh bath gels, but his days were spent in an antiseptic environment, so maybe it wasn't so surprising.

I pushed open the frosted glass door and followed him into the shower. He glanced over his shoulder, surprised, as I crowded in with him. His hair looked like molten silver plastered against his head, and his eyes were shining green as mallard feathers.

"My turn," I said.

Stephen laughed as he always did at my aggression. A little disconcerting that, but nice too. Nothing about me frightened Stephen.

"What did you have in mind, bath mitt or back scratcher?"

In answer, I presented my back to him and straddled my legs to give him easy access.

"I see." He kissed my nape, and I shivered.

He put one hand on my hips and used the soapy fingers of his other to ease his way into me. Dear God, I loved the feel of that, of his long fingers moving inside me. It didn't get more personal than that, did it? That informed press of fingertips on spongy flesh. Nothing clinical about it, nothing medicinal, just…informed.

"Yeah, you're ready," he murmured.

I moaned. I loved his cock too — although I'd never enjoyed bottoming. Good manners require taking turns, but I'd never got much out of it. It was just a way to get what I wanted. But I loved being fucked by Stephen. Loved the way it filled me up, left me with no room to think of anything but Stephen.

"You are *sweet* as a peach." He groaned, shoving into me.

I steadied myself with a hand against the wall and raised my face to the steamy spray.

I loved the feel of him all down my back, loved how hard he held me — how hard he fucked me — I could feel his heart pounding against my back, our bodies warm and wet and slippery together. I reached behind to try to touch him, to urge him closer still. He hung on tight, and I rocked and pushed back into him — a brisk, vigorous fuck to start the day.

We were panting, laughing as he turned off the taps; I opened the shower door, grabbed a towel, and handed it to him. He scrubbed the pearl gray plush against his face.

We made room for each other as we toweled off, went through the routine of shaving and brushing teeth.

“What’s your schedule like?” I asked. “Can we meet for lunch?”

“I think so. Don’t you have class today?”

“The professor’s off sick,” I said, lying. I watched myself in the mirror, watched the razor gliding up my throat in brisk, smooth strokes. No point killing myself to complete course work if I wasn’t going to be around for the final.

“I’ll call you when I know for sure.”

I nodded.

He moved past me into the bedroom. I heard the brisk slide of drawers.

* * * * *

I spent the morning going through papers, locating the shoes — the false passports — I used when traveling for The Section. I told myself I was just making sure everything was in readiness if I did decide to go ahead, but in fact it felt uncomfortably like I was making sure my affairs were in order. All that double-checking bank books, insurance documents, my will, verifying the i's were dotted and the t's crossed. I was simply making sure — if I did decide to return to the field — that everything was where Stephen could quickly find what he needed. I continued to tell myself I had not made up my mind.

I *hadn't* made up my mind. And yet when I tried to imagine telling Malik no, tried to think how I would phrase it, the picture wouldn't come. I couldn't visualize it. What I *could* visualize — only too easily — was myself on a plane.

Through the floorboards I could hear Lena Roosevelt vacuuming the study. I closed my eyes, thinking how unfair it was that I hadn't had a chance to get bored yet with these little details of domesticity. But that was just feeling sorry for myself. Embarrassing.

I finished going through everything and went downstairs with my copy of *Nicholas Nickleby* to read in front of the fire while I waited for Stephen to phone.

"Aren't you having breakfast, honey?" Lena asked, poking her head into the study. She was a large-boned but very thin black woman of a robust seventy-something. She had sharp, striking features that hinted of a mixed and intrepid heritage. She wore a brown wool dress — always dresses — and sensible shoes and iron gray hair in a tight bun. Old-fashioned wire spectacles perched on her pointed nose. I don't think she was overly impressed by me, but she adored Stephen, and so she was always briskly kind.

"I'm supposed to meet Stephen for lunch."

She studied me over the tops of her specs, nodded crisply, and withdrew, leaving me to the adventures of the idealistic and impulsive Nicholas Nickleby.

I read for a while, my stomach growling now and then. The house was redolent with the pumpkin pies baking in the kitchen. Lena was a wonderful cook, which more than made up for any flaws in her personality — such as not liking me. It was so easy to start to take all the lovely things in this house for granted; things like good food and warmth and comfortable chairs. Wouldn't be much of any of that in Afghanistan.

Stephen rang around ten o'clock.

"Bad news," he said briskly. "I can't make lunch. Hart is calling an impromptu staff meeting. He's concerned that all these sick people with costly medical conditions are messing with our performance rates and profit index."

"Right." I knew my disappointment was all out of proportion. I swallowed it down and said, "Well, I'll see you tonight then."

Something must have crept into my tone, though. I felt Stephen's hesitation, and then he said, "I'm sorry, Mark. I'm disappointed too."

"Not important." I tried to laugh and, to my horror, heard it catch in my throat.

I could hear his name being paged in the background noise. Stephen said, "I'd offer to take you to dinner tonight, but I've got that damn scholarship trustee meeting. What about tomorrow night?"

"Halloween."

"Hell. Mark —"

To my relief, my laugh sounded normal that time. "No worries. It was just a thought."

Someone came up to the phone and I heard him turn away briefly to answer a question. He came back on the line and said, "Okay. I'll see you tonight."

For nature gives to every time and season some beauties of its own; and from morning to night, as from the cradle to the grave, is but a succession of changes so gentle and easy, that we can scarcely mark their progress.

I had read somewhere that *Nicholas Nickleby* was a turning point in Dickens's writing career. It was his third novel but his first true romance. Nicholas is a hero in the classic mold: young, poor, brave, mostly noble. He gets on my nerves like no other Dickens character, including that poor little rat Oliver Twist. The novel was probably the wrong choice for my mood — *A Tale of Two Cities* would have been more like it — but I have a thing about finishing what I start.

By five o'clock, I was down to the last chapters of the novel — and no closer to making my decision — as I settled down with one of those frozen chicken pot pies and a glass of milk. I heard the front door screen bang.

I experienced another of those uneasy flashes. How had I missed a car pulling up outside the house? That kind of obliviousness was liable to get me killed when — if — I went back into the field.

I tossed the book aside and went to the front hall. Stephen, framed by the doorway, was making a fuss over Buck, who was wriggling all over in puppylike ecstasy.

"Hey, what are you doing home early?" I asked, surprised.

He straightened and came toward me. "Hi. I thought I'd take my lover to dinner." He put his hands on either side of my face and kissed me with what felt like disconcerting intentness.

When he released me, I tried to joke, "Do you suppose he'd mind if I tag along?"

But he wasn't letting me laugh it away. "You choose. Where would you like to go tonight?"

"Now I feel like an idiot. You didn't have to skip your meeting to have dinner with me, you know."

"I know. I wanted to. It dawned on me this afternoon how little time we've had together lately."

"You're busy. You've got a lot of commitments. And I've got" — I changed that in time — "one hell of a lot of homework."

He seemed to examine my face. “You’ve worked so hard these last months. I don’t think I’ve even told you how proud I am of you.”

This was much worse than being neglected. Not that he’d ever neglected me; the most he could be accused of was being occasionally preoccupied. “Don’t, Stephen. Really.” And I meant it. “I’m happy. The happiest I can remember. I wish —”

I wish it could have lasted forever.

I cut that off.

* * * * *

We ate at La Peu de Cuisine in Winchester. It was a charming little French restaurant; Stephen and I had had our first official date there nearly two years earlier. The service was, as always, impeccable, the food excellent, and the atmosphere suitably romantic: pale blue linens, crystal chandeliers, oil paintings of the Pyrenees on exposed brick walls, and large, comfortable and private booths.

Stephen had the Dover sole and I had the foie gras-stuffed guinea hen. We ordered a bottle of chardonnay from the terrific wine list, and I listened to Stephen rant about having spent the morning on the phone with flunkies at an insurance company while trying to get the necessary approval for tests one of his patients urgently needed. It was so blessedly normal that I could almost convince myself that this was how the rest of our life was going to be.

"People don't understand. Insurance company clerks are determining who can live and who dies. Insurance company clerks are playing God."

"And that used to be your job."

He glared at me, then registered the teasing in my voice. He expelled a long breath, managed a rueful grin. "It did, yeah."

"So what kind of perks does God get?"

He laughed and reached for the wine bottle. "Not enough to make up for the lousy hours." He topped my glass up.

"You don't have to get me drunk," I said. "You can have your wicked way with me anytime you like."

He grinned, very beautiful in the candlelight. I thought again how lucky I was. Even if it was all ended, I had been lucky. Most people never got close to this.

"So what did you do today?"

"Today? Today I skived off. Read mostly. Tried to teach Buck to roll over and play dead."

"Did you succeed?"

"No. He's not much for tricks."

"How are your classes going?"

"Piece of cake."

Stephen was smiling, but he sounded serious as he asked, "Are you bored, Mark? I don't mean today. I mean in general."

"No. Of course not."

He scrutinized me as though not completely convinced. "I know how quiet it is around here. How dull it must be for you. It's only reasonable that you might get frustrated, fed up."

"I'm not. I don't." I was truly startled that he could think that. It was almost funny given my idea of heaven would have been to spend the rest of my life living and loving quietly with him. In fact, I'd have taken that over heaven any day — let alone the place I was probably destined for.

"It's a drastic change from the last decade."

I shook my head. "You know better than anyone the shape I was in after that last op. I've no desire to go back."

I realized that this was the time to tell him of my meeting with Malik. To tell him what the Old Man wanted. To warn him that, desire or not, I might have to make one last run. But, gazing at his smiling face across the table, my courage failed. I knew, knew with absolute certainty that no matter when or how I broached it, such a conversation was not going to go well.

It didn't matter how hard I'd worked to prove myself over the last five months. Two years of insecurity and resentment lingered as was proved by this very conversation.

I needed to tell him, but I needed to find the right moment. The problem was that my moments were running out.

He changed the subject. "You didn't eat much dinner. Do you want dessert?"

"I was thinking we might head home. There's that pumpkin pie Lena made today."

"Ah. Pumpkin pie means fresh whipped cream," Stephen said, his grin utterly frank and utterly sexy.

My jeans were suddenly far too tight — and not from eating too much dinner.

We ran into Bryce Boxer on our way out of the restaurant. Bryce was Stephen's ex, the man Stephen had turned to when he decided I was a lost cause and it was time to move on. He was, as Stephen had told me one too many times, a very nice guy. Not Bryce's fault that I disliked him intensely. That evening he was dining with a short, stagily handsome Latino man — I pegged it as a first or second date. They were awkwardly attentive with each other.

"How are you, Bryce?" Stephen inquired, pausing by their booth.

"Stephen!" When Bryce gazed up at Stephen, his heart was in his eyes. For the first time I felt a flicker of empathy for him. I knew how it felt to lose Stephen. I'd been gutted when it had been my turn.

Bryce introduced his date, we chatted briefly, and then Stephen yielded to my silent urgings and we said good night. When we were outside on the pavement, he commented, "He seems nice enough."

"Who?"

"Alan."

Bryce's date. I'd barely registered his name. Once again I felt that glimmer of unease. I was supposed to notice things. Without trying.

"I don't think he's right for Bryce, though," Stephen was saying.

My empathy for Bryce vanished in a stab of irritation. "Why not? He seems just the type to go in for jazz festivals and Sunday brunch at the Regency Room."

"There's nothing wrong with those things."

"No. You seemed to enjoy them, certainly."

He gave me a level look. "I did enjoy them. Bryce is a caring, decent guy. And he's a lot of fun."

I laughed. I didn't mean for it to come out so derisively, but I could feel a mounting wave of aggression as it occurred to me that with me out of the way, Bryce would have a clear field again.

Stephen's expression changed. "Don't tell me you're jealous."

I mocked, "Of Alan and Bryce?"

"Of Bryce and me."

I turned my profile to him. Stared stonily at the windows of the cafes and shops we passed. "Why should I be? Or are you saying you still have feelings for him?"

"Of course I'm not saying that."

"No?" I could feel his gaze though I declined to meet it. "But you and Bryce are still friends. Even after you broke it off with him."

"Yes."

"Yet you didn't want to be friends with me."

"It's not possible for you and me to be friends and not lovers," Stephen said. "The thing between us is too intense for that."

I didn't have an answer for that; I happened to agree with him.

We continued in silence toward the car park. Farther down the street several young yobs sat on a cement wall drinking beer and yelling commentary to passing cars and the occasional pedestrian.

Stephen touched my elbow. "Let's cross."

"Why?"

He didn't bother answering.

I said coldly, "I'm not giving way to those cretins."

"This isn't the time or place for macho posturing. They're drunk and stupid and I'm not in the mood for it."

Or for me. That was clear enough.

We crossed the road and continued on our way, but as I could have told Stephen, the thugs on the cement wall recognized that evasive maneuver for what it was and were, accordingly, encouraged.

Two of them jumped down and started across the road encouraged by the jeers and calls of their mates. One of them was a big, beefy blond guy in a checked shirt, and the other was tall and lanky with a baseball cap that read Lynchburg Hillcats.

"What are you two, queer?" shouted one of the geniuses perched on the wall. He threw an empty beer can, which bounced off the bonnet of one of the parked cars.

"Hey, faggots!" called the blond ape crossing the road. "Our side of the street not good enough for you?"

Narrowly, I watched their approach.

"Oh for God's sake," Stephen said. "Just ignore them."

"I don't want to ignore them," I said, peeling off from him.

"Mark!" He grabbed for my arm, but I slid out from under his hold and advanced toward the muscle-bound point man — who'd managed to wedge himself between the bumper and fender of two closely parked cars.

The object of my interest gazed with wary surprise as I strolled up to him.

"D'you have a problem?" I inquired.

When you know how to handle yourself, it communicates itself — much the same way that fear communicates itself to a wild animal. His piggy eyes flickered uneasily at this direct approach, but he was used to intimidating people with his size, and his mates were watching, so he threw back his shoulders, blustering, "Yeah. I got a problem. I got a problem with a couple of fag —"

"I've got a problem too," I said, and I rammed the heel of my hand under his chin, which shut him up and knocked him to his knees in one swift move. "I've got a problem with not being able to walk down the street without a parcel of fucking idjits harassing me and my friends."

He was shaking his head like a bull that had mistakenly crashed into the arena wall. He tried to pull himself up. His companion joined him and tugged on his arm, saying, "Let it go, Eric. It's that crazy limey bastard!"

I recognized my friend from the fun house the night before.

"Why, hello, Bradley," I said. "I thought I told you to stay out of my way."

"You're a goddamned psycho," Eric said thickly — he'd bitten his tongue and was bleeding from his mouth.

"D'you know, I get that a lot." I rested my hands on my hips and waited, ready for someone to push his luck. Frankly, I'd have welcomed it.

Eric's face suffused with rage and he tried — though only halfheartedly — to pull free from Bradley's grip

Stephen shoved between us. "It's *over*," he warned them.

None of us needed Stephen telling us that, but I did find it mildly amusing that he apparently thought I needed rescuing. The skinny bastard was already hauling Eric — who was only too grateful for the excuse to abandon the field of battle — across the road to their comrades, who were on their feet protesting loudly the unchivalrous treatment they'd received.

"'Night, Bradley. 'Night, Eric," I called.

Stephen grabbed my arm and hustled me away; I didn't struggle.

"What the hell were you trying to do?" he was saying furiously under his breath. "You can't take on five of those assholes!"

"It wouldn't be five very long."

He stared at me in horror. I almost laughed. "I didn't mean I'd kill them," I said. "I mean they wouldn't last long in a genuine fight."

"There would only have been a genuine *fight* if you'd provoked one. They're drunken loudmouths. Why couldn't you have just ignored them?"

"Because you crossed the street to avoid them," I yelled, suddenly losing my temper. "Why the hell should *we* cross the street because of a pack of drunken loudmouths?"

His hand tightened on my arm, and he gave me a little shake. "What's the matter with you? You can't tie into every drunken bully because he offends your sense of order. Never mind the fact that *you* hit *him* first. That asshole could have you up on assault charges."

If it had been anyone else, I'd have jerked free and spelled out the facts of life for him. But it was Stephen, so I stood quietly in his custodial grasp, controlled my lousy temper, and restrained myself to a short, "It doesn't work that way, Stephen. He knows he started it whether you do or not. I was not the aggressor."

We got into the car. I stared out the window while waiting for him to start the engine. It was dark by now, and the only stars in the sky looked inferior grade and out of range. I realized that I was shaking. Not with fear, not even with anger, but from the effort of controlling myself, of controlling that tidal wave of adrenaline and aggression. Stephen was right. There was something wrong with me. I wasn't fit for civilization anymore. I didn't belong with someone like him. I didn't belong with anyone.

Why had I pretended to myself that I could do this? Why had Stephen bothered to pretend that he thought I could do this? It was like trying to cram the genie back in the bottle. I was what the years and my experience had made of me, and I couldn't stop being that just because…I wanted to. Pathetic to even try, really.

My bleak thoughts had traveled so far afield that I'd nearly forgot Stephen was sitting next to me. I was startled when he said quietly, "I do know they started it. And I know you think you were acting in my defense."

"But?" I continued to stare out the window. In the ominous green of the car park lights, I could barely discern the outline of the last ragged leaves on the trees.

"I guess what bothers me is I'm not sure if I was more worried over what they would do to you or what you might do to them."

I nodded. That confirmed my own thoughts on the matter, really. "You needn't worry about me."

"Don't I?" He drummed his fingers on the steering wheel. "One of them knew you. The one you called Bradley. What was that about?"

I considered what to tell him, mentally holding up lies and half-truths, trying to think if they would fit, and having to discard them as wrong for the occasion. I said finally, "He tried to mug me one night."

"What?"

"It's not a big deal, Stephen."

"When did this happen?"

"It really doesn't matter."

"When did it happen?" That was his medical emergency voice. *Scalpel, nurse. We have to amputate immediately.* "It was last night, wasn't it? That's why you were so wired. So angry."

"Yes. It happened last night."

I could feel him trying to read my profile in the gloom of the dashboard lights. "Why didn't you tell me?"

I said bitterly, "Don't worry. You can see I didn't do him any lasting damage."

"Mark…" he protested. "That's not what I meant. I'm not placing the welfare of those animals over you. My concern is for *you*. For what it does to you when you —"

"Lose it?"

There was a sharp silence.

"Knock off the self-pity, Mark," Stephen said, and now his voice was grim. "Your reactions aren't always in proportion, your perception of threat is sometimes off, and we both know it. If you prefer to sit there feeling sorry for yourself, I don't know what to tell you. My sole concern is for you. Believe it or don't."

He turned the key in the ignition and the radio came on. A woman's voice, husky, familiar.

Isn't it rich? Isn't it queer? Losing my timing this late in my career…

"Send in the clowns?" I nearly laughed.

Chapter Three

The answering machine was blinking when we arrived home. I instinctively knew who had left the message before Stephen reached to press the button, and I made my face blank as Malik's mechanical voice filled the front hall.

"Mark. Dicky Malik here. It appears that I'll be flying back to London sooner than anticipated. Need to know your answer, old boy." A pause and then, "I won't remind you what's riding on this."

Careless bastard. Or was he trying to manipulate me into a decision? I glanced at Stephen, and the pain on his face shocked me.

"Who's Dicky Malik?"

"Someone I used to work with."

He said nothing.

"Do you think I'm having an affair? It's nothing like that."

"An affair?" He sounded stunned. "No, of course I don't think you're having an *affair*. But something is obviously going on. Why haven't you — why didn't you just tell me?"

"I don't understand the question."

"That makes two of us. I don't understand why you're trying to hide this, whatever it is." He drew in a sharp breath. "Or am I being stupid? It's what I originally thought, isn't it? You're not happy."

"Why would you say that? I *am* happy." I could hear the fear in my voice and knew Stephen could hear it too — Christ knew what he'd make of it.

"Then what's going on? What are you doing?"

The two inevitable questions. Not like I hadn't had time to prepare for them. My mouth opened and nothing came out.

Not exactly reassuring. I could see Stephen absorbing this — the fact that I'd apparently been struck dumb — and trying to decide on the best approach. He said carefully, almost painstakingly, "I know it's not easy for you, Mark, but it would help if you could talk about what's going on. I mean that it would help *me*."

I nodded, reached out tentatively, and brushed his hand with mine. "Please. I can't bear to fight with you."

He moved his hand away. "Then stop lying to me."

"I'm not lying. I'm not ready to talk about it yet because I don't know —"

I broke off. He was shaking his head in steady repudiation — very angry but absolutely controlled.

He turned and went upstairs.

I wanted to follow him, but I was afraid he might shut the bedroom door in my face. I couldn't have taken that. Instead, I went into the study and poured myself a scotch. I knocked it back and then, out of stall tactics, went slowly upstairs.

The door to our bedroom stood open. Stephen was lying on the bed, staring up at the ceiling.

He didn't look at me, but Buck, curled in front of the fireplace, thumped his tail in welcome.

I sat on the edge of the bed, not touching Stephen. He continued to gaze bleakly up at the ceiling. I could imagine the tenor of his memories: my meltdown because he hadn't been able to spare the time to take me to lunch, then the argument over Bryce, then the near brawl in walking back to the car, and last but hardly least, the discovery that I'd been in contact with an old work mate. I probably seemed about as shaky a romantic proposition as they came.

Well? Wasn't I?

I looked down at my hands resting with deceptive calm on my knees.

"I'm losing you," I said. "I don't know what to do. Everything is" — my mouth dried so that I had to get the words unstuck from the roof of my mouth — "going wrong."

"Everything isn't going wrong."

When I glanced at him, he was watching me, his brows knitted. "What exactly were you expecting? That we would never disagree? That we would never be tired or irritable or too busy for each other?"

I shook my head. I wasn't sure I could explain — wasn't sure I had the courage to tell him what I felt was true. That I was there on sufferance, that he fully expected me to fuck up once and for all, and that, once that happened, he'd be able to cut me loose. Tell himself he'd given it every chance and it just wasn't meant to be.

More and more I had the terrible certainty that I was on borrowed time, that nothing I did would be enough to make up for my previous betrayal — and that when he learned about the impending one…

"I love you so much."

"I love you too, Mark, but it takes more than love to make a relationship work."

I waited for him to say something else, but that seemed to be all he had to say on the subject. At last I rose and went to the doorway. I glanced back, but his eyes were closed.

I thought about his expression as I sat on the sofa, sipping my second scotch and absently petting Buck.

Probably better for Stephen if I took the opening given me and gracefully departed. What had I ever brought him but trouble and heartache? For that matter, what had I ever brought anyone — barring the Old Man — but bad luck? I'd long ago outgrown the notion that I was somehow to blame myself for my parents' death — or my uncle's — but I didn't seem to be a very lucky person to love. Some people simply have that cosmic target painted on their back; I seemed to be one of them.

Was this more of the self-pity Stephen had accused me of earlier?

Possibly.

I drank some more.

It occurred to me — belatedly — that I was making an already difficult situation more difficult by not talking to him. Stephen had basically told me this himself. Angry and upset as he was, my inability to confide in him was multiplying the trouble tenfold.

Not that telling him what was going on was going to solve our problems, but *not* telling him was a guarantee of disaster.

I understood this intellectually, and yet I continued to sit there, sipping my second scotch and postponing the climb upstairs.

Not the way I'd envisioned the evening playing out. But that was my fault, not Stephen's. I'd fucked it up, and instead of fixing it — assuming that was possible — I was making it worse with every word I said. Or, more exactly, every word I'd failed to say.

It occurred to me that one reason I was afraid to have this particular conversation with Stephen was the superstitious dread that if he broke it off with me, I would have no real incentive for getting myself home alive and in one piece.

It was a new experience, realizing that I was such a coward.

I finished the last mouthful of my drink, forced myself off the sofa, and went back upstairs.

Stephen was lying on the bed. His eyes were shut, but he opened them when the floorboard squeaked. They looked red-rimmed, and I wondered if he had been crying. My heart seemed to twist in my chest. I could take anything but that.

"You're right. I have to talk to you," I said from the doorway.

He said acerbically, "That will make a nice change."

I opened my mouth, shut it.

He sat up, wiped his eyes with the edge of his hand, and said, "Sorry. That was uncalled for. It's no easier for you than it is for me. I know you're trying."

For all the good it was doing. But I put that thought out of my mind. I said, "Thursday. Last night."

He didn't look at me and his voice was flat, "The night you were late because you were getting mugged. Yes?"

No, this was not going to be remotely easy. Still hovering in the doorway, I replied, "I was mugged that night. I haven't lied to you. But I was late because I met Malik. The Old Man sent him to talk to me. He needs a favor."

I saw his face change, and it was all there: anger, cynicism, confirmation. "Yes?" That chilly single syllable could have been chipped off an iceberg. He'd been waiting for this. Waiting months for it, apparently.

It occurred to me how funny it was that I was supposedly such a brilliant negotiator that I had to be dragged out of retirement, and when it came to trying to explain myself to my lover, I could barely articulate. It was always like this when I tried to talk about the things that mattered to me personally. And about the only thing that mattered to me personally was Stephen.

So I stumbled on, trying to explain. "He — things are — the situation is critical —"

"Spare me the press release." I realized it had been easier when he wasn't looking straight at me. The black fury in his eyes caught me off guard. "He wants you to come back to work for him, and you've agreed."

To my astonishment, I heard myself say, "I haven't agreed. I won't agree unless you give me permission."

"*Permission?* Who am I? Your father? Do whatever the fuck you want, Mark. It's your decision."

I stepped back into the hallway as this time Stephen got up and left the room.

I needed to sleep, but no matter how I tried to relax, tried to empty my mind, my thoughts kept chasing round and round — like those cartoons of ghosts whirling round and round until they form a solid white ring. Like a tornado. Or a noose.

It was hours before Stephen returned to bed. I lay perfectly motionless, eyes closed, modulating my breathing. The mistake most people make when they're faking sleep is they lie too still. I felt Stephen move to stand by the bed, stare down at me, and I murmured and tossed onto my side. He pulled back the blankets and crawled in between the sheets — staying well to his side of the mattress.

For a few moments, we lay there in silence. I willed him to reach out. If he made any gesture at all, gave me any opening…

But he did not, and in a short while I could tell he was asleep.

I lay there watching the bold, gold face of the moon tangled in the trees outside the window. I watched till the moon drifted away and the stars faded and the sky paled and the sun rose.

At about six thirty I felt Stephen wake, although he didn't move.

I said, "I have to give the Old Man my answer today."

"We both know what the answer is." He sounded weary.

"It's…not just my decision."

His laugh was an echo of its normal self. "You're learning. You've memorized the right things to say even if you don't believe them."

After my struggle to reach this point of emotional epiphany, his brusque rejection left me bewildered. "I thought that was what you wanted. What you were telling me. That this had to be a joint decision."

He turned his head. Despite the fact that he occasionally fretted over the age difference between us, this was the first time he'd ever looked old to me. There were lines in his face, an emptiness in his eyes that didn't come from lack of sleep. I had done that, and it sickened me.

"It has to be more than lip service. You want to go. I'm not going to stop you."

I elbowed into a sitting position. "I *don't* want to go. I feel like I owe him. He let me walk away when I asked. He didn't have to do that. He could have —"

Stephen sat up too. "You don't have to explain. I told you last night I understand how boring all this is after the life you've led."

"No. You don't understand. This — what I have with you, what we have here together — is exactly what I want. What I dreamed of."

He said impatiently, "Then why are you throwing it away?"

"I'm not. If I do this, it's because I have to, not because I want to. And it will be the last time. I promise you that."

He threw back the covers, got up, reaching for his maroon bathrobe. "You promised once before, yet here we are."

"I couldn't foresee this."

"That's funny. I could."

"Stephen…don't."

Maybe he heard the pain in my voice; I couldn't conceal it. Certainly I could hear the pain in his as he cried, "What do you want from me?"

What *did* I want from him? Besides reassurance that if I did this, it wasn't at the expense of our life together. And how could he guarantee that? I was ashamed to even ask.

When I didn't speak, he said in a voice of goaded frustration, "Jesus Christ, Mark!"

He slammed into the bathroom, and I went downstairs to put the coffee on.

A few minutes later I heard him and Buck on the staircase; then Stephen called from the hallway, "I'm going for a run."

"Be careful," I said automatically.

He didn't answer.

The house was uncomfortably silent after they left.

On weekends Stephen permitted himself a big, cholesterol-laden breakfast, and I placed bacon in the frying pan, moving automatically around the kitchen, trying to analyze my situation objectively, strategically.

It seemed to me that at least part of what I was fighting was Stephen's own insecurity about us. Astonishing as it was, he was genuinely uneasy about the twenty-one year age difference between us, failing to understand how much I needed his centered maturity, how attractive I found his assurance, his wisdom, his — usually — unruffled approach to life.

From the first time I'd seen him, smiling across the ugly, flaming centerpiece at some tedious State Department dinner, I'd wanted him — loved him, if there was such a thing as love at first sight. If anyone had grounds for insecurity, it was me. The last time I'd screwed up, Stephen had done his level best to replace me with good old Bryce Boxer. In fact, if I understood the situation correctly, the only reason Stephen had let me back in his life was because good old Bryce had basically insisted that Stephen needed to work out what he really felt for me before they could be together. I had Stephen because Bryce was foolish enough to send him back to me.

Bryce would be only too delighted to pick up the pieces this time.

As for our life being boring…

That was like arguing that warmth and light and love and happiness were boring. Suffice it to say, I'd had all the excitement anyone could handle for one lifetime.

But although this was all very clear in my mind, I didn't know how to communicate it to Stephen. I thought I *had* communicated it. Maybe not in words. I wasn't particularly good about explaining my feelings, but surely he could tell in every other way?

Somehow — I had to figure out how — I had to make him understand this in the little time we had left.

When he came back from his run, his hooded sweatshirt was wet from the fog.

"Coffee's ready. Lena left a jar of apple butter for the toast," I said. "Did you want your eggs fried or scrambled?"

He poured dog food into Buck's bowl and said carefully, "Actually, I was thinking I'd go into work."

My mouth dried. "I thought you had today off."

He said something I didn't catch.

"What?"

"I'll be home for dinner." He went on through, his feet pounding on the staircase as he jogged upstairs.

I found myself unable to call after him, form my protest. We had so little time left.

Less than I'd thought. What had Dickens said? Life is made of ever so many partings welded together.

I put the frying pan on the floor next to Buck's dish, grabbed my jacket, and walked down to the lake.

Chapter Four

It had been a long day. A long day and a bad day.

The phone rang several times, but I didn't pick up and no one left a message. When it rang at four, I heard it out, waited for Stephen's voice to tell me he wasn't coming home, but once again there was only silence.

Stephen arrived a few minutes later bearing a bottle of wine and Chinese takeaway.

"Trick or treat." He kissed me briskly on my startled mouth. Cool and minty fresh. I loved the clean, male taste of him.

"Trick?" I inquired doubtfully, watching him set the little cartons on the tile counter.

He shook his head. "Treat. Happy Halloween."

"I'd forgotten all about it."

"Not a big holiday where you come from. Why don't you open a bottle of wine?"

I felt a bit like a sleepwalker as I opened the wine, poured it into two glasses. I handed Stephen his glass.

Meeting my eyes, he said wryly, "You look like you think I might have booby trapped the egg rolls."

"This morning you weren't speaking to me. Tonight it's Mongolian beef. I can't help wondering if this is the condemned man's hearty last meal."

"No." He sipped the wine, swallowed. "I'm sorry about this morning. I've got a heck of a lot of nerve lecturing you about talking and then walking out on you. I just…needed time to think today."

I braced myself for it. "And?"

His gaze held mine. "I'm not going to hold you to the promise you made me. If you feel this is what you have to do, then" — he drew a deep breath and expelled it slowly — "I accept that."

It took a second or two to absorb that my first and foremost reaction was sick disappointment. I realized that I'd hoped he would refuse to let me go. That he would deliver an ultimatum, somehow come up with a legitimate reason for why I couldn't leave. All day I had put off phoning my answer to the Old Man in hope of this.

I didn't let myself show any of that, though. I said, "And assuming I survive, will I have a home to come back to?"

He said quietly, "Don't joke about not surviving. Do me that much of a favor."

I'm not joking. But if he was as worried as he clearly was, he didn't need to hear my own fears.

I got plates out of the cupboard and spoons from the drawer. We sat down at the table, dished out the food. Stephen talked about his patients and the med center while we both picked our way through the Chinese food.

It was completely normal and utterly weird.

Stephen said suddenly, as though feeling his way through a maze, "Do you feel I'm neglecting you?"

"No."

But he was thinking this over. "I have been busy, but..." Whatever he read in my expression changed his own. He said uncertainly, "Maybe this is partly my fault. I've been trying not to smother you, making sure you had plenty of time — room — to be confident that you aren't making a mistake."

Protecting himself in case I bailed on him once more. Yes, I understood that.

I said, "I don't think you believe me when I say I don't want to go. I'm not bored or frustrated living here. I was happy. I *am* happy." He opened his mouth, and I headed him off. "Maybe you're right and I'm having some problems adjusting to civilian life, but...I *want* to adjust. I want to teach. I want to be your lover and wake up with you every morning and go to sleep next to you every night. I *want* what we have here."

Stupidly, I was getting choked up again. It was with relief that I heard the doorbell ring, although in my experience, doorbells ringing unexpectedly at eight o'clock at night rarely signal anything good.

I half rose, but Stephen reminded me, "Halloween. I'll get it."

Was he afraid I might lose it and blow away the little ghosts and goblins invading our front porch?

After yesterday evening, he probably was.

Buck and I followed him to the hall where we could watch. A chorus of high voices cried, “Trick or treat!”

And so it began. Over the next several hours, I watched Stephen handing out gobs of autumn-colored packages of candy to swarms of kids. He was terrific. I’d never had even the slightest paternal inclinations, but it gave me a funny, warm feeling watching Stephen with his little neighbors. He admired costumes and made bad jokes all the while handing out ungodly amounts of sweeties.

Had he wanted kids? Was that one of the sacrifices he had made in order to be true to who he was? There was still so much I didn’t know about him.

The ghosts and goblins and miniature Transformers eventually trickled off and stopped. Stephen turned off the porch lights.

He finished off the last of the wine and I drank my scotch as we sat in front of the fire in the study.

“Did you want to go up?” he asked, and I realized I’d been miles away, staring into the flames.

I gazed at him, and his expression seemed odd to me. As though he were waiting for something. What?

“I’ll lock up downstairs.”

He nodded and left me to it. I went through the house checking windows and doors, turning the lights off, locking up.

I had felt good earlier, watching Stephen with the kids. Now I felt drained and melancholy. As though I were doing all this for the last time, saying good-bye to the house and the all the things in it, which was silly because Stephen had promised me that I could come home again, that I was not leaving for the last time.

Bryce would not be stepping into my shoes, but I wondered who would remember to lock Stephen's doors and windows with me gone. Who would take care of him? It wouldn't occur to Stephen that he needed taking care of too. Or that I was the person to do it.

The bedroom light was on, Buck dozing in front of the fire, Stephen sitting up in bed. He wasn't reading, though; his arms were folded across his knees, and he was staring out the window at the moon in the magnolia branches.

I stepped out of my jeans, tossed them to the antique hope chest at the foot of the bed, pulled on my flannel sleep pants. He dragged the blankets back for me, and I slid in beside him on sheets warm and scented of him.

He turned out the light. I felt something close to a wave of panic that we were just supposed to close our eyes and go to sleep, but to my relief he reached for me. I went to him gratefully, holding him tight. He stroked my bare back.

"Did you call him? Malik. Or Holohan? Whichever it is."

The last thing I wanted to talk about. I shook my head, face pressed to the hollow of shoulder and arm. He smoothed his hand down the curve of my spine, his touch lingering over the shifts of muscle and bone as I tried to control my breathing.

He said slowly, "You're shaking."

I tried to laugh.

"You *don't* want to go, do you?"

I shook my head.

"Then why the hell are you going?"

"I..."

He sat up, dislodging me, and turned on the light. I put my hand up belatedly to shield my eyes.

He said tautly, "Why are you going, Mark? Why are you doing this?"

"I owe him."

"Bullshit." He said it so fiercely I fell silent. "You gave him ten years. For ten years you risked your life and sanity for him. You've been beaten, stabbed, shot. How the hell do you figure you owe him another minute more?

"He's fighting for his political survival."

"His political survival? Against your life? *Our* life. No. That's not an even exchange. You don't owe him a goddamned thing more. He was your employer and he used you until you weren't of anymore use, and then he cut you loose. And you think because he let you keep your pension — that we don't need, by the way — he did you some great favor? Anything he did for you, he did because it was convenient to him."

Partly that was true. Partly...no. But I didn't argue it with Stephen because he was getting angrier by the minute without my help.

"Why?" he demanded again. "It was one thing when I thought you wanted to go, but —"

"Because I don't deserve this."

I'm not sure who was more thrown by that outburst. Stephen's eyes did a funny little triple blink as if the information was coming into his brain too fast to process. But he questioned calmly enough, "What do you mean?"

"You know what I mean. You know what I *am*. You said it yourself."

"Mark —" Whatever he had been about to say, he cut off. In that other voice, the quiet, calm voice he said, "I know what you did for a living. Is that what you mean?"

All at once I was so tired I couldn't see straight. I rubbed my eyes and said, "I don't know. Do you think it's a coincidence?"

"What?"

"Everyone I love dies."

"Mark, you can't honestly think — yes, for the record. I do think it's a coincidence. Sad, tragic, and…inevitable. Because we all die."

"You know what I think? I think you're right. I think I'm not fit for civilized society."

"I never said that."

I closed my eyes.

"I never said that. I don't believe it for one minute. You did the things you were ordered to do because you believed you were helping to make the world a safer place, that you were protecting the people who needed and deserved protecting."

"That the ends justified the means."

He said with complete certainty, "You don't believe that. You've done things you don't want to talk about, but you did them because you believed there was no other choice."

He sounded absolutely positive about this, which was especially strange given that earlier in the evening I'd been thinking there was so much about each other we didn't know.

Maybe not the important things, though. Maybe we did know those things.

"You are *not* one of the bad guys."

I opened my eyes, scrutinized his face, tried to see if he really meant that or not. "And I don't know anyone who values peace, who understands how fine the line is between chaos and civilization more than you."

"Yesterday evening," I began.

"I don't know that your instinct was wrong," Stephen admitted. "I know that like most people, I'm slow to recognize danger signals, that *my* instinct is to avoid violence, not meet it head on. Not escalate it. I was afraid for you. I'm afraid for you now. That's why I was — and am — angry."

I considered this uncertainly. Afraid for my physical welfare or mental welfare or spiritual welfare or all of the above? Did it matter? He was right to be worried. I was.

Stephen said, “Did you sleep at all last night?”

“No.”

He gathered me against him again. “No wonder you’re talking nonsense.”

Not nonsense, though. Nice of him to pretend that it was, but it wasn’t, and we both knew it.

Stephen continued to hold me. *Cradle of arms*. Where had I heard that phrase before? Sentimental twaddle. But lovely too. I suppose he thought I might sleep, but as exhausted as I was, I couldn’t let go enough to sleep. I needed to get up and make my phone calls. The last obstacle had been removed. Stephen would accept my decision and at the end of the job would still let me back into his life. So this was victory. This called for celebration.

I lay there dry-eyed and hollow.

What use would I be to the Old Man — to anyone — as I was? Didn’t anyone see that I was different now? That I *had* changed? I’d lost my edge — filed it down in an attempt to live safely with Stephen in his world — and now it was gone. Even Stephen, who knew me better than anyone on earth, apparently did not see this fundamental truth. Maybe it didn’t exist. Maybe I hadn’t changed at all.

Safe to say the world had not changed. I closed my eyes. Listened to the steady pound of his heart, the slow breaths — as peaceful as when he slept. He wasn't sleeping though. He stroked my hair.

Finally — I have no idea how much time passed — I whispered, "What if I did just choose this?"

"What?" He lowered his head to better hear me.

"If I do have a choice, can't I choose this?"

"Yes."

He said it immediately as though…as though there were no shame in it, as though he wouldn't think worse of me for shirking my duty, for letting down a friend — for letting down the Old Man, who had been so much more and so much less than a friend.

"*Yes*," he repeated as though he himself didn't have serious doubts about us, about the wisdom of letting me back into his life.

He wasn't judging me; not his style. But I wanted him to understand that it wasn't just funk. That the decision was at least partly practical. I said, "I'm so *tired.* I don't think I have what it takes anymore. I'm not…absolutely sure I could…make it back. If I risk leaving you again."

His arms went so tight around me, I gasped. But when he managed to speak, his voice was even, quite calm. "I'd say that pretty much answers the question, wouldn't you? You're not going anywhere."

There was a prickle at the back of my eyes.

"No? I don't think it can be this simple. I don't think I can —"

"*I* can," he said flatly. "I can and I will. It will be my pleasure." He sounded very Southern. I almost laughed except I wasn't sure it would be laughter. Stephen was the only person in the world who thought I needed protecting.

Did people like me get happy endings? Doubtful. It was hard to steady my voice. "Do you think we're going to make it?"

He paused too long before saying, "Do you?"

"I feel like I'm…" I had to stop. I tried again, and it was easier with my eyes closed. "I feel like you don't believe in…" This? Us? Me? "That you're going through the motions because it's the fair thing to do, to give me a chance to see for myself that it won't —"

"*What*?"

I opened my eyes at the affront in his voice.

"What the hell are you talking about?" Before I could answer he went on, "You think I'm doing this, *living with you*, on a trial basis? What would be the purpose of that?"

I started to speak, and he said — sounding decidedly pissed off — "If we don't make it, it will be your choice, Mark. Your decision. Not mine. I'm in for the long haul. As far as I'm concerned, this is *it*."

The few times I'd tried to imagine having this conversation, it hadn't gone like this: with Stephen offended, even outraged at the idea that he wasn't fully committed to making it work. But then he would think that, wouldn't he? Even if I was right? He would certainly be giving it —

"No," he said flatly, and my eyes jerked to his face. "Whatever you're thinking, whatever you've convinced yourself of, no. You're not here on sufferance. I love you. I love you so much it scares me. It's not reasonable to care this much for anyone, but…I do. And believe me, if it was possible to talk myself out of it, I'd have done it long before I ever let you move in here. There's nothing I wouldn't do for you. Christ, I've killed for you. And I'd do it again. I *love* you."

I clenched my jaw against the emotion threatening to tear out of me, wrapped my arm around his neck, and buried my face against his throat.

"I love you," he said again, very softly against my ear. "And I'm not letting you sacrifice yourself. Not to Afghanistan, not to an ex-lover, and sure as hell not to some noble ideal. So say good-bye to the past and all those ghosts who have you convinced that you don't deserve to be happy." His lips found mine, a soft kiss on my tight mouth, and my own lips relaxed. I kissed him back.

And as tired as I was, I realized that I wasn't *that* tired. That there was, in fact, life in the old boy yet.

Stephen glanced down at the prod of my erection and smiled a slow, gentle smile. His hand moved down to free himself and then me, and his equally hard cock slid against my own.

I kissed the thin skin of his neck, nipped delicately as Stephen responded, then harder. I could feel him smiling as his mouth trailed hot and silky, leaving a trail of wet from throat to nipple. He licked me, his tongue rasping against the sensitive points, and I gasped. When it was good between us, it was wicked good.

The bed springs *pinged* as he shifted around, and when I pried my eyes open, he was crouched over me, his breath warm on the head of my cock.

I spy with my little eye…

"You don't have to do that," I said quickly.

"You always say that," Stephen said. "I never understood why. I thought you were the only guy in the world who didn't like it. Well, guess what? I like doing this for you. So you're just going to have to get used to being loved."

His mouth closed on my cock, hot, wet, luscious. He began to suck me, taking my swollen, pulsing prick deep in his throat.

Say good-bye was about right. I arched my back and cried out — and wondered dimly if they heard me all the way to London.

Acknowledgments

Thank you to Chris Quinton for the Brit-check

I SPY SOMETHING CHRISTMAS

Josh Lanyon

"Men's courses will foreshadow certain ends, to which, if persevered in, they must lead," said Scrooge. "But if the courses be departed from, the ends will change."

Charles Dickens, *A Christmas Carol*

Chapter One

I don't trust any man who says if he had the chance to live his life over, he wouldn't do it all differently

Right. Maybe not all, maybe not everything, but if I had it all to do again, I'd make bloody well sure I woke up fewer times in hospital. Although finding Stephen sitting at my bedside was some compensation for the pounding head and throbbing shoulder.

"How do you feel?" His voice was low, his green eyes dark and unsmiling.

I nodded, licked my lips, got out, "Brilliant. What happened?"

I rather thought I knew what had happened, seeing that it wasn't the first time it had happened—so Stephen's terse, "Someone shot you," wasn't the shock it might have been. Or perhaps should have been.

"You're going to be fine," Stephen added reassuringly. He probably needed the reassurance more than I did. This wasn't routine for him. Actually, it wasn't routine for me either anymore, not since I gave up the spy game seven months ago and settled down so Stephen could make an honest man of me.

"I'm all right." I squeezed his hand and he squeezed back.

The room was as dark as hospital rooms get—not particularly dark—so it was clearly very late. The window across from the bed offered a view of lightless night. Now and again white splotches hit the glass and vanished. It was snowing again.

After a time it occurred to me to ask, "Who shot me?"

"You don't remember?"

I put a hand up to my head. There was a plaster over my left temple, and stitches beneath the adhesive bandage. "No. What happened?"

Stephen was watching me closely. "That's what the campus police and the sheriff's office would like to know."

"It happened at the university?"

"Yes. Outside the library."

"Was anyone else hurt?"

"No."

I waited for him to go on, but he said, "I'm not supposed to discuss it with you until you've given your statement."

Confusing. Very.

"It's going to be a brief statement. The last I recall I was sitting inside Smith Library reading."

"I see. That's the official explanation?" Stephen sounded very Southern Gentleman. His face gave nothing away, which in itself was a tell. My heart sank. I'd hoped the old distrust and disappointment were behind us.

"It's the only explanation."

He didn't believe me. He was too polite to say so, what with my being injured, but I was getting to know Stephen pretty well by now.

"I don't lie to you, Stephen."

He nodded. He still held my hand, so I preferred to concentrate on what he was communicating by touch. His thumb feathered across my knuckles. *Shhh. Shhh now…*

My head was thumping away in time with my heartbeats. More than anything I wanted to close my eyes and forget my troubles for a while. But that was not an option.

I said, "When can I get out of here?"

"Honey, you're not going anywhere." Stephen sounded definite on that score. "You've got a concussion. They're going to keep you at least forty-eight hours for observation and tests."

"No. Not necessary."

"It's absolutely necessary."

"I'm not spending the night here. I hate hospitals."

"I know," Stephen said dryly. "It's a little awkward, me being a doctor and all."

I sputtered a laugh and sat up gingerly. I couldn't have been too concussed since I didn't keel over again, but the blood thudded in my temples and my stomach gave a dangerous lurch. I was out of practice, that was the trouble.

Stephen let go of my hand and stood over me. He put his hands on my shoulders—my good shoulder anyway—trying to press me back against the pillows, but I wasn't having any of it, and he wasn't prepared to wrestle me down. "Mark, this is idiotic. It's after midnight."

"Then it's high time we were home and in bed." I held my arm with the IV out to him. "Will you do the honors or shall I?"

He swore under his breath then gently, deftly, unhooked me. I stood up, gripping the bed rail for support.

"Mark—"

"I know. Can you take care of everything? Fill in the forms? Talk to whomever you have to talk to."

"It doesn't work like that!"

But it did and we both knew it. "Stephen, I need your co—help. I can't sleep here. I want to go home." That was true, but more to the point, until I knew what had happened to me—and why—I needed to be on my own turf where I could more effectively assess and respond to potential threat.

Stephen said again, helplessly, "Mark." He did not often sound helpless.

"I'm all right. Truly. Or I will be once we're home." I offered what I hoped was a conciliatory smile. Stephen reached out to steady me.

"This is crazy. You need to get back in that bed. Now."

I pulled away from him, though it was the last thing I wanted to do. It was a little unsettling the way Stephen brought out in me a desire to let go, to lean. "Where are my clothes?"

He sucked in a breath and I forestalled the imminent explosion. "Stephen, you're a doctor. I couldn't be in better hands, right? I'll recover much faster at home."

"Sit down," he ordered. "Don't move until I get back."

I obeyed, sitting on the edge of the bed and holding my hands up to illustrate perfect compliance. He left the room. I closed my eyes and concentrated on not falling over. I felt completely and utterly wretched, but it was all right now. Things were in motion. Stephen would handle everything. It was one of the things I liked best about him; he was a man who got things done. If he said he would do a thing, there was nothing left to do but make out the report. It was a trait I had valued highly in my previous line of work, but it was just as useful in civilian life.

The door opened and Stephen was back. I wondered if there would ever come a time my heart didn't lift at the sight of him. He was a fit and handsome fifty: tall, lean, long legs and broad shoulders. Tonight he wore jeans and a tweedy blue-gray sweater that made his eyes look blue and his hair platinum.

"That didn't take long."

He gave me an unamused look and handed over a plastic bag. "Your personal effects."

I put on my watch and the sterling earring Stephen had given me for my last birthday, while he retrieved my jeans and boots from the cabinet against the wall. "They cut your jacket off. Your sweater and your tee shirt, too."

"Hell. I liked that jacket. I'd only just broken it in."

Stephen pulled his sweater off, and when I started to object, gave me a glinting look. "Ta," I said meekly.

I managed to dress without falling over—something Stephen was clearly waiting for—and we crept out into the silent and sterile hall.

The nurse at the floor station gave us a disapproving look. "Doctor," she said primly.

"Nurse." Stephen sounded equally forbidding, which made me smile. He kept his arm around me. I didn't really need the support, but I didn't mind it, either. We got into the lift. The light was hard and unflattering. It seemed to carve grooves around Stephen's mouth and nose.

"You look tired," I said.

"I am tired."

"I'm sorry I put you through this."

He shook his head as though there was no response to that, and perhaps there wasn't.

Christmas music was playing quietly in the lobby when the lift doors opened. An orchestral version of "Blue Christmas," my all time least favorite Christmas song. We went past the displays of children's art: lop-eared reindeer, deformed Santas, and menorahs that looked more like instruments of torture; past the towering and tacky gold Christmas tree; past the closed gift shop, mechanical toys bobbing their heads on the window shelves; past the weary front desk personnel, and out through the automated glass doors.

The snow had dissolved to a slushy rain. Stephen hustled me across the slippery car park, unlocked the black SUV, and helped me inside. The rain rattled down like nails on a tin roof.

He climbed into the driver's seat, started the engine and turned on the heat. The radio blasted on as well, a local news station.

I pictured Stephen's drive to the hospital. *Sorry, Stephen.*

He turned off the radio. The windscreen wipers squeaked across the glass.

I shivered. Stephen said, "Are you sure you're up to this?"

"Of course."

He shook his head, but he put the vehicle in motion.

We didn't talk. It was late, the driving conditions were poor, Stephen was weary. Not the time for a chat.

I wracked my brain, tried to remember…but it had been an ordinary day. A day like any other. Saturday. The first day of the winter break. It was always quiet at the weekends, but that day the campus was like a ghost town with most of the students and staff already away on holiday.

I'd had an uneventful and informal afternoon meeting over coffee with my advisor and, knowing that Stephen would be working late, I'd decided to stay and study in the campus library.

And that was what I'd done. The last clear memory I had was of trying to ignore my growling stomach—I hadn't bothered with dinner—while reading a particularly dull paragraph on classroom audio systems.

After that…nothing.

“They shot me twice and didn’t manage to hit anything vital?” It wasn’t really a question. I was mostly thinking aloud, thinking that it was either an amateur or a warning. Except there was no reason for anyone to warn me off. I wasn’t involved in anything.

“They?” Stephen inquired.

“Assuming, that’s all.”

“Assuming what?”

“Not sure, really.”

Stephen’s terse tone told me he believed I was prevaricating. “You were shot once. In the shoulder. Not much more than a graze. You hit your head when you fell. That’s how you got the concussion.”

“I fell?”

Stephen nodded. “The walkway was wet and slick.”

“Blimey.”

The miles rolled by and Stephen’s grim muteness began to impinge on my consciousness. Belatedly, I thought again about what a hellish shock he must have had when he got the phone call that I’d been shot. The original Bad Boyfriend. That was me.

It was more than shock, though. I could feel his tension, his…anger? No, not anger. Worry, yes. But more. Suspicion.

I broke the lull. “Stephen, I give you my word I’m not involved in anything.”

“And if you were, you couldn’t tell me anyway.”

“I would tell you. We agreed. No lies between us.”

“We did agree.”

"But you think I'm lying?"

I could feel him weighing his words. "I think if you thought it was safer—safer for me, certainly—you'd withhold information. I don't suppose you'd think of it as lying."

"Give me a little credit."

I didn't like the silence that followed my words. Stephen said at last, "We don't need to talk about this now. You're feeling like hell whether you want to admit it or not. I'm not giving you any ultimatums."

"Marvelous."

He must have heard the bitterness in my tone. He said painstakingly, "I love you, Mark. Nothing changes that."

But he was hurt and disappointed.

As was I. Despite all we had been through, despite the last months of domestic tranquility, Stephen didn't trust me.

A blue Christmas indeed.

Chapter Two

Flannel sheets, soft, warm duvets, down-filled pillows. Would I ever take these homey comforts for granted? I didn't think so. So much of my life seemed to have been spent in sleeping bags, on rocky ground or sitting upright, back to the wall and pistol in my lap. Lying back in bed felt like sinking into a cloud.

"Thank Christ," I muttered, closing my eyes. Home safe and sound. My shoulder gave a twinge. Safe anyway.

"How's the head?" Stephen asked from somewhere overhead.

"Fine."

"Shoulder?"

"Fine."

"No, Buck," Stephen said sharply, and I heard Buck's nails scratch the wooden floor as he was shoved away from the bed. I didn't have the energy to open my eyes. Stephen, again close at hand, said, "I can give you something if it will help you rest."

"No need."

He moved quietly around the bed, shifting the pillows behind my shoulder, straightening the duvet. Not fussing. Stephen wasn't a man who fussed. He was a man who understood pain and had made it his life's mission to alleviate it where he could.

"Better?"

I assented without words.

He turned out the light. I said, “Don’t go.” I opened my eyes.

“I’m not going anywhere.”

I watched his silhouette undress, neat and quiet, and then he climbed in beside me, careful not to jar the mattress. He needn’t have worried. This bash on the head and creased shoulder were nothing. I’d had much worse.

He settled a considerate few centimeters away. I reached out, tugged his wrist. He eased his way over and we wrapped our arms around each other. I buried my face in the curve of his neck, breathed in his scent. Before Stephen I would never have believed antiseptic and mouthwash could provide such a sexy base note to a bloke’s aftershave.

“Thanks for breaking me out of the nick,” I mumbled.

He shook his head and made a huff of sound. Not quite a laugh, but softer than exasperation.

We lay quietly and our breathing slipped into a natural synchronized rhythm. It felt like our hearts were beating in time. Only with Stephen had I ever experienced this feeling of completion, of oneness. I could have gladly closed my eyes and slept in his arms—was desperate for sleep—but I could feel him thinking, feel his thoughts turning over and over.

I said at last, “It kills me that you don’t believe me.”

“Mark,” he said at once, so I knew I had been right, “if you tell me you don’t know who shot you, then I believe you.”

"Yeah. Except you don't."

I could hear him thinking that through, hear the steady deliberate beat of his heart, hear the slow even breaths. He said at last, "It's hard to believe you wouldn't have any idea at all."

"It's not hard to believe if I'm not involved in intelligence work."

"But if you're not involved in espionage, why would someone try to kill you?"

It was a good question. A fair question.

"Maybe I…"

"What?"

I said vaguely. "Dunno. Not everyone appreciates my winning personality the way you do."

"Who've you offended badly enough they might want you dead?"

"No one that I know of." Not recently at least. I needed to talk to the Old Man. There had been a price on my head for a brief time, but that was ancient history. True, it wouldn't be advisable for me to return to Afghanistan in the near future, but I hadn't been shot in Afghanistan. I'd been shot in what amounted to my own back garden.

"Weren't there any witnesses?"

Stephen's head moved in negation. "We can't keep discussing this. Not until you've talked to the police."

I lifted my head from his shoulder. "You what? To hell with that."

"No. We're liable to compromise your memory of what did actually happen."

I said irritably, because graze or not, I don't enjoy being shot, "I don't bloody *have* a memory of what happened."

"There's a good chance you'll get at least some of that back. You're trained to retrieve information even under the most stressful circumstances."

He was right about that. I'd been knocked senseless a couple of times and I'd always recollected everything right up to the moment of losing consciousness.

I resettled my head on his chest. "I think it would help me to talk about it."

He laughed, though it wasn't a particularly humorous sound. "I let you have your way at the hospital and I'm going to catch hell from the cops for it. This, we're doing my way."

When he got that note in his voice there wasn't any arguing with him. And in any case, the last thing I wanted was to row with him.

I sighed. "All right then. You win."

He promptly reached up to feel my forehead. I managed a tired laugh.

"I hope at least you believe I wouldn't knowingly do anything to bring trouble to us."

"I do."

Turnabout was fair play though, because I didn't believe him any more than he had believed me earlier.

"But you reckon I believe I could protect us from any trouble that might result from my activities?"

"Mark, we're both too tired to hash this out now." Stephen's voice dragged with weariness. "We'll talk when we've both had some sleep."

"All right."

Another heavier silence settled over us.

Stephen said suddenly, "We should probably cancel the party."

A few days earlier Stephen had broken the news that every Christmas Eve he hosted a party for his friends and colleagues and the people with whom he served on all those endless charities and committees. Something like eighty people had already RSVPed. Stephen had hired a bartender and caterer so that Lena, our housekeeper, was not subjected to what, in my opinion, promised to be an excruciatingly dull evening.

"Why?"

"Aside from the fact you didn't want this party *before* you were shot?"

"I'll be as good as new by tomorrow. As for not wanting a party, I can dust off my manners for one evening."

I could feel him thinking that over.

I said, "You know me well enough to know I'm not merely being polite."

"True."

This time the quiet felt as though it might stick. I made myself lie still and I felt Stephen relaxing, his breaths going slower and deeper.

My head pounded and my shoulder felt stiff and bruised. But beyond the physical aches and pain was the nagging worry of who wanted me dead? Wanted me out of the way so urgently as to risk attacking me on a college campus? Fair enough, it had been night and the campus was largely deserted now that winter break had begun, but it was a hell of a gamble.

On the whole I was glad the shooter had tried for me safely away from home base. The one thing I couldn't bear to contemplate was Stephen getting in between me and a bullet. Not that I had any desire to stop a bullet, but I'd gladly stop a dozen bullets to keep Stephen out of the line of the fire.

But bullets shouldn't be an issue these days. I wasn't telling Stephen comfortable lies. I genuinely had no clue as to why anyone might view me as a problem that was best solved permanently.

Stephen said quietly, "Can't sleep?"

"It's all right. I don't need anything."

"Nothing at all?" His voice was deeper, his drawl was a little more pronounced.

That caught my interest. "What did you have in mind?"

"I'll show you. Just close your eyes and relax."

Stephen's hand closed around my cock, warm and familiar. *Hello old friend. How are you?*

I arched into it—I'd have to be in a coma not to respond to Stephen's touch.

"Shhh. I'll do all the work."

"Feels so nice..."

"I know." There was such sweetness in his voice, such tenderness. It made my eyes sting. I kept my lashes tightly shut and focused only on his touch.

His hand slid up and down my cock, slowly, skillfully. The right pressure, the right speed, the right angle. That delicious pull and tug, the friction of palm on penis. Maybe it wasn't skill so much as knowing by now exactly what I liked. He knew my body as well as he knew his own. The same way I knew and loved his body.

"So good," I murmured. "Thank you."

I heard the smile in his voice as he whispered, "The pleasure is all mine."

That was certainly not true, but I'd learned enough these past months to know that a *lot* of the pleasure was his, and that it was okay to accept this gift without instantly needing to reciprocate and repay. It was better to give than receive, but receiving had its delights, too.

Even tired and battered as my body was, it responded with quick efficacy to Stephen's attentions, and before long I was gasping and shoving hard into his fist, all that worry and tension spiking and then pouring out in slick, wet heat.

So good, even as reaction hit. I was shivering as Stephen wrapped me tightly, warmly in his arms, kissed my damp temple, my damp eyes, my unsteady mouth.

"Sleep well, honey. You're safe now."

A wet tongue in my ear.

The wrong tongue. My eyes flew open. "Damn it, Buck!"

Buck made that growly sound that was the Chesapeake Bay retriever way of saying hello. His big brown eyes gazed hopefully into mine.

"What?"

Buck wagged his tail. He growled encouragement.

"Sorry, mate. You only get one breakfast when Stephen's home."

Through the floorboards I could hear sounds of life and activity. Muted sounds, no doubt in consideration of my delicate condition, but there was nothing wrong with my hearing. I heard the oven door opening and closing in the kitchen, the stereo in Stephen's office turned down low but not so low I couldn't make out Darlene Love singing "Baby Please Come Home," and the distant drone of a utility vehicle making its way down the snowy lane toward us.

I lifted my head. The clock read nine-thirty.

Stephen had been up since five. I had pretended to sleep through his shower and getting dressed because I knew he'd be fretting if he thought I wasn't getting enough rest, and in my effort to convincingly feign sleep, I had drifted off again and slept well.

To Buck's delight, I threw back the covers and proceeded to get myself carefully and cautiously out of bed. On a scale of one to ten, I was scoring a solid five. My head hurt but my vision and balance were back to normal. My arm hurt too, but I could move it fine. I picked at the dressing on my shoulder and took a peek. Red and angry looking as it was, it was just a nick, as Stephen had assured me. There was a lot of bruising, by which I deduced I'd fallen on it.

Buck escorted me to the bathroom, his face falling as much as a dog's face could fall when I closed the door on him. I wrapped my head in a towel to protect my stitches and got in the shower, washing quickly and mostly managing to avoid getting my injured shoulder wet.

I followed the shower with a shave, brushed my teeth, and found a clean pair of jeans and a gray Henley shirt. I knew I didn't have a lot of time. I could hear voices downstairs, official sounding voices.

I sat on the edge of the unmade bed and phoned the Old Man but the number I had, the number I'd always had, rang and rang and rang.

"Who were you calling?" Stephen asked from the doorway.

Buck jumped off the bed with alacrity, but there was no reason for me to jump, no reason for me to feel guilty at all.

I did, though.

I replaced the phone in the cradle. “The Old Man. Just making sure no one put a price on my head.” I offered a smile. Stephen didn’t smile back.

The sense of well-being I’d awakened with, well-being at least as far as Stephen and I were concerned, paled.

“The sheriff is downstairs.”

I nodded.

“How are you feeling? How’s the head?”

“Fine. Shoulder, too.”

“I want to check you over, but I think you should talk to him first.”

“Whatever you like.”

I saw him struggle with himself. “What did Holohan say?”

“He never answered.”

Stephen’s brows drew together. “You mean he’s not taking your calls?”

I offered a wry smile. “I mean no one’s answering.”

“What does that mean?”

“Maybe they haven’t paid the phone bill.” I rose and went to where he stood in the doorway. I sensed he wanted—started—to kiss me, but he stopped himself, and that dimmed my spirits a little further. “I suppose I’d better get this over with.”

He nodded and turned away.

I've interfaced, as we say in the service, with a lot of law enforcement. They run to type as do we all, but I couldn't immediately pinpoint Deputy Sheriff Donleavy's type.

He looked to be in his late forties. Medium height, wiry, and sharply handsome. When we walked into the front room, he was examining the framed photos of Stephen and me which sat on the top of the piano in front of the large windows. He turned to greet us without haste and introduced himself.

We settled near the fireplace. I sat on the sofa, back to the ten-foot tall noble fir that dominated the room. Stephen sat across from me. Donleavy took the catacorner loveseat, giving him the best vantage for watching both Stephen and me.

"How are you feeling, Mr. Hardwicke?" He accepted a cup of coffee from the tray Lena had carried in.

"Fine. Thanks." I smiled at Lena in gratitude for the cup of tea also on the tray.

Her face softened before she turned to leave the room, snapping her fingers for Buck to follow her, which he did reluctantly, with longing looks at the tea tray.

"You had a pretty close call there last night."

I swallowed a mouthful of tea. "Yes."

Stephen had neither coffee nor tea. He watched me and Donleavy gravely. I knew he was too smart not to realize he was, for now, a suspect in the attempt on my life. I could only imagine how outrageous and offensive that idea was to him.

Donleavy said, "You want to tell me in your own words what you remember?"

"I'm afraid I'm not going to be a lot of help."

"I'm afraid of the same thing," Donleavy said dryly.

"Sorry?"

He took a biscuit from the tray. "Your professional background is not completely unknown to us, Mr. Hardwicke. Simple country cops though we may appear to you."

"I've worked with a lot of different agencies, Deputy. I have the greatest respect for local law enforcement."

His smile was dazzlingly white. "Sure you do. Since we've got the niceties out of the way, suppose you tell me what you're working on that got someone riled enough to try and put you out of the way?"

"Nothing. I'm telling you straight up. I'm not involved in anything more dangerous than teacher training." I looked at Stephen. He looked right back at me. "I retired from British Intelligence seven months ago. I have no intention of getting back in the game."

"Okay." Donleavy crunched his biscuit thoughtfully. "So who do you think wants you out of the way?"

The fact that Donleavy accepted my statement without argument took me aback more than the question itself.

"I can't think of anyone. Maybe it was a mistake."

"A mistake? You mean someone thinks they have a grievance but they don't?"

“No. Maybe someone thought I was someone else.”

“A case of mistaken identity?”

“I have that kind of face.” I shrugged. “I look like a lot of other people.”

“That’s an interesting theory. Of course you don’t *sound* like a lot of other people. Not in this neck of the woods, anyway.”

“Was I talking when I was shot?”

Stephen threw me a warning look, but I wasn’t being insolent. I thought it was a valid point.

Donleavy said, “Were you? Did you leave the library with someone?”

“I don’t remember. The last thing I recall is sitting inside the building reading. I remember thinking it was late and I should be starting home.”

“Memory loss isn’t unusual with head trauma,” Stephen interjected. “But Mark is trained in memorization techniques. I think it’s likely he’ll remember most of the events up to the shooting after he’s had a couple of days to recover.”

“That would be useful,” Donleavy said, not sounding particularly wowed at the possibility.

“Were there any witnesses?” I asked.

“To the shooting? No. A couple of students left the library a minute or so after you and found you trying to push yourself up from where you’d fallen. They didn’t see anyone else. You lost consciousness and one boy ran back inside the library for help while the other stayed with you.”

“Was the bullet found?”

“Nothing so far. No bullets. No shell casings. It appears there was one shot at a distance from a rifle, probably a twenty-two.” Donleavy turned to Stephen and said, “Dr. Thorpe, just for the purpose of—”

“I understand,” Stephen said. “I was on duty at Shenandoah Memorial yesterday evening. Any number of people will be able to vouch for me.”

Donleavy nodded. “People never like that question, but I have to ask all the same.”

“I did not shoot Mark.”

“No, sir. I don’t believe you did.”

“If he had, he wouldn’t have missed.” I wasn’t being funny. It was a fact. But both of them looked at me like I’d said something extraordinary.

To me, Donleavy said, “Have you had any altercations lately? Any run-ins with anyone?”

“No.”

“No? You get along with everyone, is that it?” He offered that big smile again. His eyes were arctic blue. “Everybody loves you?”

“No. But I can’t think of anyone who doesn’t love me enough to want me dead.”

Or did I?

Observing me, Donleavy queried, "I guess the light bulb went on?"

"Er…no."

"Mark," Stephen said sharply. "If you can think of someone who might want to harm you—"

I don't think it was malicious on my part. I wanted to distract Stephen from the memory of the last real altercation I'd had, and the best way to do that was to sidetrack him with another option. Donleavy needed a bone. I threw him one.

"I don't know that he wants to do me harm, but Bryce certainly doesn't wish me well."

"Bryce?" Donleavy asked at the same moment Stephen exclaimed, "*Seriously*, Mark?"

He was furious and not bothering to hide it behind his usual good manners, which indicated how really pissed off he was. Not on Bryce's behalf necessarily; Stephen was a reserved and private man, not given to sharing intimate details of our life—his life—with strangers, and I had just ripped the door off his safe room and turned on a spotlight. I hadn't intended to embarrass him; I hadn't considered that angle at all.

One glimpse of his face warned me I should have. By then it was too late to turn back.

"And who might this Bryce be?" Donleavy inquired.

Stephen stopped trying to raze me to ashes with his eyes long enough to clip out, "A family friend."

"There seems to be a difference of opinion there." Donleavy waited for me to clarify.

I tried to minimize the damage. "Bryce and I have never really got along, but I don't actually think he's got it in for me. I'm not thinking too clearly this morning."

"No, you're not," Stephen said.

Donleavy was a smart bloke. He didn't need a diagram drawn. "What's Bryce's last name?"

"Boxer," I replied, now annoyed myself.

Stephen gave me a stony look.

Donleavy asked a few more pertinent questions, but I had given him the lead he needed, and about ten minutes later he left with a promise to keep us apprised of his progress.

I let Stephen see him to the door, not because I wasn't feeling well. I simply wanted to postpone the inevitable argument. I didn't have long to wait.

"What the hell was that about?" Stephen demanded, returning to where I sat finishing my tea. He didn't bother to sit down. "Why would you do that, Mark? Why would you accuse Bryce of all people?"

"I don't know," I said. "I suppose I was flustered. I couldn't think of anyone else."

"Flustered? *You?* Bullshit." His eyes seemed to snap with anger. "You did that on purpose."

"Oh, right. I'm so vindictive—or is it paranoid?—I'd rather set the law on your ex-squeeze than help the plods figure out who tried to kill me."

"You can't think Bryce shot you!"

The more Stephen defended Bryce, the less sorry I was for throwing his former boyfriend to the wolves. "I've news for you, Stephen. Everyone, every one of us, is capable of killing under the right set of—" I remembered who I was talking to and under what circumstances Stephen had been driven to kill, and I shut up.

Not in time. Stephen's face was colorless. "I'm late. I should have been at the hospital half an hour ago."

"Stephen."

He left the room without another word and went to the hall cupboard to get his overcoat. I followed him.

"Stephen, I'm an idiot."

He slipped on his coat and picked his briefcase up from the hall table. I thought he wasn't going to speak to me, but at last he said, "You need to take it easy today. Rest."

I didn't want him to leave while we were on these terms. I stepped in front of him. "I will. Stephen, I'm sorry."

He had his normal color back and his eyes were no longer angry. But there was something in their expression I liked as little as I'd liked the anger. Sadness? He said, "I know. I'll be home for dinner."

When he hesitated, I made the move to kiss him. It wasn't smooth but we managed to latch mouths without breaking noses or knocking any teeth out.

"Ow," Stephen said, rubbing the bridge of his nose.

"Damn." I put a hand to my lip.

He made an exasperated sound, somewhere between a sigh and a laugh, and drew me forward again. An efficient yet unexpectedly gentle kiss.

"I'll see you tonight." He closed the door quietly.

Chapter Three

Most of the denizens of the Jubilee Manor Estate had spared no expense in decking the halls—and roofs, car porches and lawns of their mobile homes—for the holiday.

Number 213, home to Bradley Kaine, stood in stark and unadorned contrast to his neighbors.

I knocked on the door. There was no answer. The lights glowed behind brown curtains and I could hear the unmistakable sounds of video game gunfire. I thumped harder with my gloved fist.

The door opened and the man himself stood framed against a backdrop of cigarette smoke and gloomy interior. Emaciated body in dirty jeans and a brown plaid shirt, stringy hair, unshaven face.

"It says No Solicitors!" he informed me on a gust of beer-breath that could have knocked down his neighbor's plastic reindeer.

"No worries. I don't plan on suing you. I may, however, shove your teeth through your brain."

It took a full twenty-nine seconds before recognition dawned on his narrow face.

"You're that crazy limey bastard!"

"That's me, mate. And what are you? I'm thinking inept, wannabe assassin."

"H-h-huh?" Kaine fell back into his abode which I felt could be construed as giving permission to enter. I followed him inside. The interior smelled of tobacco and bad plumbing. The TV offered a frozen image of a man being killed execution style by another man in a black hood. There was nothing remotely realistic about the dead man's expression, but the blood spatter pattern was accurate enough. Stacks of unopened DVD players and boom boxes blocked most of the hall leading to the bedrooms. DVD players and boom boxes? So three Christmases ago. Kaine wasn't any smarter a thief than he was would-be murderer.

I opened a couple of cabinets, checked inside cupboard drawers. "What are you doing?" Kaine demanded, backed up against the wall. "What do you want?"

"You better get wrapping, Bradley." I nodded to the tower of stolen electronics. "Only two days 'til Christmas."

His eyes did a weird jittery shift as though he were about to have a seizure. "What do you—I'm not—I'm storing them for a friend."

"Of course."

"Why are you here?"

I kept searching. No gun rack. No guns. No weapons at all unless you counted a couple of kitchen knives. Of course the rifle might be out in his car. I stopped prowling and had a good long look at him. He was an unlovely sight. A pale, weasely face: close-set muddy eyes; a small, wet mouth; lank, greasy, dark hair. He was terrified, which was to be expected. And totally bewildered, which wasn't.

Maybe he was a better actor than I gave him credit for. Or maybe I was out of practice reading villains.

"Who'd you hire to try and kill me? I want the name and address."

"W-w-what?" He actually swayed like he was about to faint. "What are you talking about?"

No, he wasn't that good an actor. He was genuinely, blankly confused. No clue as to what I was talking about. None.

I'd been so sure.

But I'd been wrong.

Kaine hugged himself and struggled not to cry. His frightened eyes never left my face.

Awkward, this. Very.

I said, "Someone tried to kill me last night. I thought it was you."

"Me?"

I nodded.

"Are you." He swallowed and had to start again. "Are you going to kill me?"

I stared at him hard. "Did you try to have me killed?"

"No! No! I swear to God. I swear on a million Bibles. I never did."

"Then, no. I'm not going to kill you."

An instant of relief, then his expression grew more wary. Too much telly. I sighed. "I'm not going to hurt you. I'm not going to do anything to you." I moved to the door of the mobile home.

He took a pace forward. Stopped. "You're just going to leave?"

"You can lock the door after me."

"How do I know you won't come back?"

"You don't. So keep your nose clean."

His Adam's apple jumped as he swallowed. He put his hand up to the organ in question. "My…nose…clean?"

"Don't break the law." He glanced instinctively at the mountain of hot merchandise. I said, "I'd dump that lot at the nearest Oxfam, if I were you."

He opened his mouth. Closed it.

I said softly, "I see you when you're sleeping. I know when you're awake. I'll know if you've been bad or good. So be good for both our sakes."

He was standing there motionless as I closed the door behind me and stepped out into the snowy day.

I heard him scrabbling to bolt the door behind me.

Not Bradley Kaine, then. I had been so sure.

If not Kaine, who?

Thoughtfully, I walked back to my car, my boots crunching in the snow. Though it was still afternoon, the mobile park street lamps were coming on and Christmas lights burned in windows. It smelled like wood smoke and pine trees. The sky overhead was leaden and heavy. More snow on the way.

I'd been living an entirely blameless life for the past six months. There was no reason for anyone to want me out of the way. I was no longer privy to state secrets. I was not involved in any operation or enterprise that might get my head blown off. Not until I actually had my teaching degree and entered the classroom.

I pictured Stephen's wince at my saying such a thing aloud. It was a violent world, right enough. But it didn't have to be. If there were more men like Stephen and fewer like me…

But back to my own immediate concerns.

The last person I'd had any sort of run in with was Bradley Kaine.

But that dog, as Stephen might have put it, would not hunt.

Where did I go from here?

I reached the car, unlocked it, and climbed inside. Resting my arm on the steering wheel, I stared out at the snow-draped trees and considered my next move.

As hard as it was to believe, it had to be someone from the past. But anyone from my past wouldn't have missed their mark. Anyone from my past would have finished me last night, not delivered a flesh wound and fled.

I drummed my fingers restlessly.

And then the idea came to me. So obvious I was astonished I hadn't seriously considered it until now. I'd even thrown it out to the local cops as a decoy.

I did stand in the way of one person.

Bryce Boxer.

* * * * *

Bryce lived in a townhouse on Hisey Avenue in Woodstock. Stephen and I had been to dinner at his house twice. Once would have been plenty for me, but Bryce kept asking us and Stephen couldn't seem to figure out a polite way to say no. Apparently *Mark doesn't like you* wasn't sufficient.

A wreath of poinsettias hung on the white door. The windows were painted with snowflakes.

Like Bryce wasn't getting enough snow these days?

I used the shiny brass knocker and in short order the door swung open to the sound of Perry Como and the scent of baking.

"Mark!" Bryce smiled at me in surprise. A Santa hat perched on his thinning fair hair. He wore a reindeer-patterned apron. "Is Stevie with you?" He peered past me.

It occurred to me that I had to use a little restraint here, a little decorum. If I was wrong about Bryce, *Stevie* would have my head on a platter. So I smiled my most charming smile and said, "No. I was doing some last minute Christmas shopping and I thought, as I was in the neighborhood, I'd stop by."

"Oh." He did his best to hide his disappointment—and his puzzlement. "Well, come in! Come in! Have a cookie and a glass of eggnog."

"Thanks."

I stepped inside and had a glimpse of myself in the oval mirror that hung in the entryway. Medium height and lightly built, dark hair and razor smile. Nothing to identify me beyond the white square of bandage on my forehead and the unobtrusive silver earring. It didn't matter. Even if Bryce had tried to kill me, I wasn't going to harm a hair on his thinning head. I knew Stephen would never get over that. I would find another way to deal with it.

But it had not escaped my notice that, like Bradley Kaine, Bryce seemed neither guilty nor alarmed to see me on his front step.

He turned his back to me, leading the way to the kitchen, raising his voice to be heard over the music, "I'm surprised to see you running errands, Mark. I couldn't believe it when I saw the news last night. Another shooting. What is this world coming to?"

"I don't know."

The living room looked like a bomb had gone off in a craft shop. There were garland and candles and fairy lights and shiny beads everywhere. Several handmade stockings hung from the white fireplace mantel. It looked like someone had tipped a treasure chest over a squat Douglas fir struggling to stay upright beneath the weight of glitter and glass.

Bryce went straight into the kitchen and hauled a couple of trays out of the oven. The smell of vanilla and butter and sugar reminded me that I hadn't eaten all day.

"Sit down," Bryce told me. "I'm making snicker doodles. I can't believe you're not in the hospital. Although I guess Stevie…" That trailed off. I don't suppose he wanted to picture Stephen soothing my fevered brow. He said instead, "Do the police know who tried to kill you?"

"They've got a pretty good idea." It was clear to me that Donleavy had not yet interviewed Bryce. Slack. Very slack. But then again, maybe Donleavy was busy checking Bryce's background and potential alibis. Maybe Donleavy knew something I didn't.

"That's a relief!" Bryce spared me a quick smile, busy using a spatula to free the snicker doodles from the baking sheets and dropping them onto cooling racks. "Was it another student?"

"Another student? Why would you say that?"

"It happened at the college, didn't it? I just assumed it would be a student."

I was watching him quite closely and I saw absolutely no flicker of fear. No sign of guilt or deceit. No, qualify that. When Stephen's name came up, yes. Bryce felt guilty about what he still felt for Stephen and he did his best to hide his feelings. But beyond that? No. Nothing. In fact, he was apparently so clear of conscience that it had yet to occur to him that anything sinister lay behind my impromptu call.

He wasn't stupid, though. Stephen couldn't have cared for a stupid man. And he had started to care for Bryce before I stumbled back into his life. I gazed around the kitchen and couldn't help a flash of depression at the thought that maybe this—maybe Bryce—would have made Stephen happier than I could.

The tinsel and snicker doodles and Perry Como, that was all Stephen. Okay, maybe not the reindeer apron. But all the rest of it…I couldn't help but think there must be times when Stephen wished for something less…tiring.

Yes, that was what had been in his eyes that afternoon. The same thing that had been in his voice last night. Weariness.

There must be times—times like last night—when Stephen wished for something less complicated. More snicker doodles. Fewer bullets.

I couldn't blame him for that.

I tuned back in as Bryce set a glass of eggnog before me. "I make it myself, from scratch."

Of course he did.

I said, "Thanks." Bryce watched wide-eyed as I drained the entire glass. It was unexpectedly delicious. "I missed my lunch," I offered in explanation.

He started toward the fridge "Let me get you another. Or I could make you something—"

"No. Thank you. I ought to be on my way."

"But you just got—"

He turned back to me and I could see that he was beginning to put the pieces together. He was flushed and his eyes were too bright.

"I see. You just wanted to stop by and say hello."

"Yes." I rose. "Thank you for the drink."

"Let me send some cookies with you at least."

"Thank you, but that's not—"

Bryce said tersely, “I insist.”

Oh hell.

“Thank you then.”

Bryce got out a tin decorated with Scotty dogs and red plaid. He began to fill it with cookies, his movements stiff and jerky.

I watched him for a moment and an unfamiliar impulse seized me. I said, “I remember now. I was supposed to make sure you’re coming to the party tomorrow night.”

An unfamiliar and highly stupid impulse.

Bryce said shortly, “I RSVPed with Stephen yesterday.” He gave me a bleak look and thrust the tin of cookies at me.

I took the cookies and nodded thanks. Bryce did not speak on our way to the front door. I found I was all out of brilliant ideas.

Bryce opened the door.

I said, “So we’ll see you tomorrow night then?”

He nodded tightly. Perry Como was singing “That Christmas Feeling” as the door shut in my face.

* * * * *

“Where the hell have you been?” Stephen shouted when I unlocked the front door and let myself inside our house.

“I—” I hadn’t expected him to be home early, let alone find him standing in the front hall waiting to greet me. I use the term “greet” loosely. “Kill” was probably more accurate.

"Lena had no idea where you were. I thought maybe you went back to the university to poke around, so I called security. I was just about to call the sheriff's."

"You…" His eyes looked black in his white face. Clearly he had been terrified. Terrified for me. The idea that he thought I couldn't take care of myself was so ludicrous, it surprised a disbelieving laugh out of me.

A most serious error.

Stephen's face realigned itself into lines I'd never seen. "You think it's funny?" His voice was so quiet I could hear the sudden resounding silence from the kitchen where Lena was working. Baking gingerbread, from the smell of it.

"No. I don't think it's funny. I'm sorry you were worried. It didn't occur to me that you'd be alarmed. I thought I'd be back before you were home."

He didn't hear the last part of that. Didn't hear more than *it didn't occur to me*.

"It didn't occur to you? Someone tried to kill you last night. Someone *shot* you. And according to you, you have no idea who. You don't think that would worry me? That wouldn't occur to you?"

"I can take care of myself, Stephen. You don't have to worry about me." Not that his worry didn't touch me, but—

"Two months ago you didn't think you could survive another mission. But I'm not supposed to worry when after an attempt on your life you disappear for five hours without a word?"

He was right, of course. As usual. That didn't make the reminder of my previous vulnerability any more pleasant. In fact, I began to get irritated, too. It wasn't as though I hadn't been good at my job. Too good for his taste, as I recalled.

"Look, Stephen. I'm sorry you were alarmed. I apologize for that. But I'm not a child or a mental defective. I can take care of myself."

"Obviously. You did a great job last night."

I had never thought I could be truly angry with Stephen, but live and learn. "I'm still standing here, aren't I? What I don't need is you coming the heavy father and phoning around town checking up on me."

Even as the words were leaving my mouth I knew I was making a bad situation worse. I saw the words hit home, saw Stephen's expression change again, and I remembered too late his insecurities about the age difference between us.

"If you don't want me to act like your father, then stop acting like a self-centered child, Mark," he said without emotion, and turned away.

"Hang on!"

He ignored me and went down the hall and into his study. Buck gave me a mournful look and trotted after him. The door closed behind them.

Chapter Four

The whispered sound of the study door closing seemed to echo down the hall like the crack of doom.

In the kitchen, I heard Lena open the oven and noisily pull out a rack.

My upsurge of aggression drained away and I was left to wonder what the fucking hell was the matter with me? Of course Stephen had worried. His was the normal reaction.

I strode down the hall to his study, then hesitated. I seemed to be getting a fair number of doors closed in my face today, but I couldn't remember Stephen ever shutting me out.

Maybe he meant it.

Forcing him to deal with me when he wasn't ready could make everything that much worse. I'd negotiated enough deals in my time to know that better than anyone. But the idea of being shut out by Stephen was intolerable.

I opened the door.

He stood at the window staring out at the frozen lake and the magnolia trees with their snow blossoms. He didn't turn, though he couldn't have missed the door opening or Buck's tail thumping in greeting.

"That wasn't the right reaction," I said.

Stephen continued to gaze out the window. "It was an honest one."

"What I mean is, you put me on defense and I overreacted."

"True. But that's not the point, is it?"

I wasn't sure what he meant. What was the point? For me the point was I shouldn't have said what I said. "You were right. I was in the wrong. I apologize."

He made a sound, a smothered sound, but of such pent up frustration that my heart froze. That level of irritation and exasperation wasn't the result of one argument; it had built up over time. Was he ready to give up on us? Probably.

I said desperately, "I know I'm bad at this, Stephen."

He turned then. He looked older, grimmer, as though he'd aged in the time it had taken to walk down the hall.

"Yes. You are. It's not enough to acknowledge it, Mark. You have to make an effort to change."

"I'm trying."

"Are you? Is that what today was? You trying to turn over a new leaf?"

I hadn't felt this panicked, this sick since the last time I'd returned from Afghanistan to realize that Stephen had stopped loving me, had moved on.

I tried to think of what to say, but I knew that anything I came up with would seem to him like I was trying to find excuses instead of taking responsibility. Or maybe taking responsibility was another thing that was beside the point. Not only did I not have the answer, I wasn't sure of the question. What did he want? Whatever it was, I was more than willing to give it, if it was in my power. But it increasingly felt like trying to argue a court case in a language you had only the feeblest grasp of.

He continued to stare at me in that dark, measuring way.

I went on reviewing all the possible responses he might wish from me, but staring at his face, listening to that formidable silence, I was forced to conclude that it wasn't a matter of what he wanted, it was a matter of what he expected. And what he expected was my agreement with the conclusion he had apparently already reached.

"I thought things were all right between us," I tried.

He shook his head.

Wrong again, Mr. Hardwicke.

I said finally, dully, "It's too much work, isn't it?"

Since he hadn't said a word to me in minutes, I didn't see how the room could get any more hushed, but it did. Stephen didn't move a muscle. The stillness surrounding him was absolute. As absolute as death. At last he said, "Is it?"

We were wavering on the edge of the world and the earth was crumbling out from under us. Nothing but black space and jagged stars below. It was surely too late, but instinctively I grabbed for whatever was left. "Not for me. Never for me. I know I keep fucking up, but surely…it can't be as bad as it was in the beginning."

He said carefully, as though he was a blind man feeling this way through strange surroundings, "What is it you think I'm saying to you?"

"You've had enough. Had all you can take."

The life came back to his face. “Mark.” I couldn’t tell if that note in his voice was tenderness or pity, but he was coming to meet me and we held each other for a fierce moment as though we really had just missed plunging off the edge of the world. “Honey.”

He wasn’t much for endearments. Neither of us were.

Buck, curled in front of the fireplace, stirred his tail in approval.

Stephen’s voice was warm against my ear. “Mark, listen to me. We’re not going to separate because we get mad at each other and argue. Getting mad and arguing is part of being with someone. Even someone you love as much as I love you. Do you understand that?”

I drew away. Of course I understood intellectually what he was saying. I told myself the same thing when we rowed. The problem was we didn’t argue much and when we did it was inevitably something serious. Maybe it was a shame we didn’t bicker like a lot of other couples, because I’d have more practice and wouldn’t take it so seriously.

“For better, for worse,” I said.

“Right. Our commitment to each other is a…a safety net. It allows us to be honest, even if we’re honestly angry, without fearing we’re going to tear apart.” He was as earnest and careful as someone explaining the rules of conduct to someone from another land.

The earnestness made me smile. Stephen sighed, but his eyes were amused. “What’s funny?”

I shook my head. "Just relieved. I know we've had this talk before, but I keep expecting you to give up and hit me over the head with the nearest blunt object."

"That's not going to happen. The giving up, I mean. No guarantees about the blunt object."

We kissed again.

Catastrophe averted. Stephen didn't ask me what I had been doing while I was out and I didn't volunteer. The entire subject was dropped. He would find out soon enough that I had visited Bryce, and he would not be pleased. We would argue, but now I understood that we would not break up over it.

It was a wonderful feeling, a feeling of great freedom. Until now I had tried to ensure that every argument was our last, certain that lack of conflict was the best, maybe the only way to guarantee the survival of our relationship. But at last I understood that Stephen did not expect our relationship to be free of conflict, and that our commitment to each other was mutually shared.

Given the fact that I still had no idea who had tried to kill me, I was curiously happy that evening. My heart felt as light as a snowflake.

The closest I came to addressing anything perilous was as we were finishing dinner. "Did Donleavy phone while I was out?"

"No." Stephen hesitated. "Were you able to get hold of Holohan?"

"Not yet."

Stephen nodded and refilled my wine glass. "Dessert?"

"Mm. What if we had it upstairs?"

He smiled. "Great idea."

First, though, he insisted that we go downstairs to his examining room so he could check that my shoulder and head were healing properly.

"Only the good die young," I teased after he reluctantly pronounced that I was on the mend.

"You do realize how lucky you were?"

"Every day."

He sighed and turned away to wash his hands at the little sink. I unpeeled myself from the tissue on the examining table and got off the table to hug him. I wanted to reassure him yet again that I wasn't involved in anything dangerous, but I knew he realized by now that I wouldn't be poking around and asking questions if I were yet engaged in skullduggery.

From upstairs came the slow, somber chime of the grandfather clock.

"Eight o'clock. All's well. Come to bed," I said.

* * * * *

Stephen needed to take the lead that night, and I was glad to let him. Glad to let him feel in control, glad to let him take comfort in my compliance, glad to let him know he was not alone, that everything he felt, I felt, too.

Every day, every hour, every minute with him mattered to me. I never wanted to take one instant of our time together for granted.

He used his weight to hold me down, pushing me into the mattress, covering me with heat and muscle. My body quivered with tense anticipation. Stephen's hand gripped my hip, and I reached to cover his big hand with my own, encouraging him. Stephen's free hand cupped my chin. He plundered my panting mouth.

I opened to his kiss, and Stephen's mouth was sweet and hot, going from needy to passionate to voracious. "Whatever you want," I whispered. "Anything you want."

He growled deep in his throat. I laughed, but it made my stomach flip, too. I loved his aggression. I felt for his free hand, lacing my fingers with his. "I love your hands," I told him. Strong hands. Gentle hands. The gentleness of true strength. Healing hands. They had healed me. Not just my body, my spirit.

"I love touching you," Stephen replied. He slid his leg between mine, rubbed his hot, hard thigh against my balls, pressing his knee into the sensitive strip of flesh between sac and opening. I moaned. It takes a lot of trust to let another bloke put his knee in your crotch. I spread myself wider.

Stephen groaned in echo. We both started to laugh. He shook his head. "God. What you do to me." His hand slowly kneaded its way up my flank, my waist, ribs and chest, exploring in massaging strokes that changed from firm to gentle and back again.

I squirmed. "Oi! Tickles!"

"Does it?"

"Bastard."

Stephen was still laughing as he kissed me again. I loved the taste of his laughter. Loved when he sealed our mouths together once again, claiming me with a fierce possessive strength that made my heart hammer against his rib cage. My cock thrust up, throbbing, leaking, aching for release.

Stephen's face quivered with emotion; I think, somehow, it surprised him that I needed him as much—probably more—than he needed me. He met my urgency with his own controlled hunger, probing at my lips until I opened to his tongue. We kissed deeply, passionately, then Stephen withdrew to press the corner of my mouth in tiny chaste touches, teasing the nerves in thin skin, trailing his lips to my nose, grazing my eyelids with delicate, ghostly touches.

There had been a time in my life when kissing—if it happened at all—had merely been prelude to the performance. The means to an end. Now it was an end in itself, and one of the loveliest improvisations in the world.

Though the succeeding movements were nothing to complain about. I rolled over, burying my face in my arm. Stephen took great time and care in his preparation before at last accommodating my desire and his own, parting my arse cheeks with a sort of tactful proficiency and pushing in deep.

I responded with needy grunts, writhing on my belly, hands twisted in the pale flannel sheets. Stephen gripped my hips, taking charge, thrusting possessively into me in long, smooth strokes.

"Yes. Jesus, yes....Stephen...."

The slick heat of him sliding in and out of my body...I pushed up to receive the hard, rhythmic thrusts Stephen delivered. I wanted to take him in deeper still, shivering with that instinctive blazing clutch of muscle and nerves. That ingrained human need for union, to couple, to be one, even if only for a short while.

"You. Are. So. Sweet," Stephen panted, each word punctuated by a hard, quick stroke.

Stephen changed his hold, angled his thrusts to hit the swollen nub inside my tensed body. Helpless desperate sound came rolling up from my guts to spill out in inarticulate noise, something between pleas and praise. Amazing. Bewildering. To feel so much. So much it didn't seem my heart could hold it all. Fire blazed at the core of my abdomen, an electric buzz of slow building, blissful ecstasy, all bright lights behind my eyelids and constricted muscles in my chest and belly as orgasm crept up my spine.

Stephen arched and stiffened, changing to short strokes, plunging his cock frantically, fiercely into my taut body. He was coming too; I was aware of it in the wake of the fireworks exploding in my head. Roman candles and Chinese rockets and bells ringing out. Christmas and New Year all rolled into one. I was dimly aware of the pulsing beats of Stephen's emptying cock. The wounded, winded sounds he was making in my ear as we collapsed together, clutching each other, hot and wet and sticky, into a welcoming darkness.

Soft light behind my eyelids.

Music was playing downstairs. Bing Crosby. Very traditional. I smiled. The floorboard squeaked and I opened my eyes to soft light and smells of Irish coffee and warm gingerbread.

Stephen, naked beneath his navy dressing gown, set the tray on the bed and crawled in beside me once more.

"You're spoiling me."

"Lena is spoiling us both." He broke off a piece of gingerbread and held it out to me as though he were feeding me wedding cake. I raised my head, nibbled the gingerbread, licked his fingers when I'd taken the last bite. He closed his eyes and gave a twitchy smile. I kissed his fingertips and let my head fall back in the pillows.

"Favorite Christmas carol?" I asked.

"Modern or traditional?"

"Both."

"'Silent Night.' 'Please Come Home for Christmas.' You?" He offered another bite of gingerbread.

I took a bite. Swallowed. "This year? 'I'll be Home for Christmas.'"

He smiled, understanding. "Traditional?"

"Not really a carol. The Christmas section of Handel's *Messiah*."

"I should have guessed that. My turn. Favorite Christmas movie?"

"Mister Magoo's Christmas Carol."

Stephen laughed.

"Quite serious. It's one of your classics, yes? I loved that razzleberry dressing and woofle jelly cake."

"You do enjoy your food. I'm not sure where you put it." He stroked my ribcage.

I sucked in my stomach. "Yours?"

"It's a Wonderful Life."

I said, "You've made a difference in a lot of people's lives. A good difference."

His green gaze was grave. Sometimes he saw too much. "Best Christmas memory?" he asked.

"This," I said. "Tonight."

* * * * *

The Old Man had retired.

It took me half the following day to discover that piece of intelligence—ours was one of the most hush hush of organizations in British intelligence—and another couple of hours to track him down.

"Well, well. If it isn't the Ghost of Christmas Past," John Holohan acidly greeted me when I finally managed to locate him at his country house in County Mayo. "Happy Christmas, Mr. Hardwicke."

I'd forgotten it was already Christmas Day, there. No wonder it had taken forever to negotiate the halls of power—or, more correctly, the channels of officiousness.

"Happy Christmas, sir."

"To be sure. You've no doubt heard the news the bastards've put me out to pasture. That's the lump of coal I found in my Christmas stocking. Forced retirement. 'In the public interest.'"

"I'm sorry, sir. They're bloody fools."

He cleared his throat. I could see him in my mind's eye. Tall and rawboned, a shock of white hair and a beaky, fierce face like a bird of prey. Though he was in his late sixties he'd always had the strength and vitality of men half his age. I imagined it was no different now and knew how bitter a pill this redundancy must be to swallow.

"Indisputably. So you see, if you've thought better of your unwise decision to retire—"

"No. I'm happy where I am."

"You were always an odd lad."

"The issue is whether someone else might not be as happy about my retirement?"

"I don't follow you." He sounded genuinely bemused.

"Someone tried to take me out a couple of nights ago."

The silence seemed to echo across the cold, gray Atlantic.

"Whatever have you got yourself involved in, Mr. Hardwicke?" the Old Man asked softly.

"Nothing that I know of. That's why I wondered—"

"Whether Her Majesty had sent someone to twep you?"

He needn't have sounded quite so entertained by the notion.

"No?"

"No one even remembers you, Mr. Hardwicke. Let alone is interested enough to fill in the forms required to remove you from this mortal coil. No, whoever you've annoyed to the point of homicide isn't being paid for the privilege of sending you to meet your maker."

"What about Istakhbarat? They came after me once."

He made a dismissive noise. "Mullah Arsullah came after you. He's dead. Istakhbarat is gone. Look to your own doorstep, Mr. Hardwicke. If someone does want you dead, they're hiding in your backyard."

As the gloom and shadow thickened behind him, in that place where it had been gathering so darkly, it took, by slow degrees, - or out of it there came, by some unreal, unsubstantial process - not to be traced by any human sense, - an awful likeness of himself!

"Maybe Holohan's not in the loop anymore," Stephen's reflection interrupted my reading. We were sitting on the sofa before the fireplace. Or rather Stephen was sitting. I was stretched out with my head in his lap. He was listening to music and scratching my head. I was reading *The Haunted Man*—I take turns reading one of Dickens' Christmas stories every year—in between dozing. Nothing puts me to sleep like having my head rubbed. That light, knowledgeable touch sent exquisite tingles over my scalp and down my spine. "Maybe he doesn't know, but he doesn't want to admit it."

"He'd know," I said sleepily.

"He'd like you to think so. It might not be true."

I blinked up at him. "They've only just shoved him out the door. Besides, he's right. I'm no threat to anyone. I'm not even a person of interest anymore."

Stephen's mouth tugged into a wry curve. "You're of interest to me."

I smiled. "I like to think so."

"So what now?"

Apparently we were going to have this discussion whether I was awake or not. It would be better to be awake. I shook off my pleasant lethargy. "Maybe it was an accident. Maybe I was simply in the wrong place at the wrong time."

Stephen's mirrored expression was one of disbelief.

"There haven't been any further attempts. Besides, if someone was out to get me, I'd surely have some warning."

"That's just in the movies, isn't it? Threatening letters and death threats spray-painted on your car?"

"That stuff, yes." I was thinking more that I'd know if I'd done something to seriously piss off someone. I'm not *completely* lacking in social awareness. I was also thinking that part of how I'd managed to stay alive as long as I had was my built in sense of self-preservation. I'd had no sense of being watched or stalked in the days or even the hours before I'd been shot.

Stephen looked unconvinced.

"The sheriff's department hasn't come up with anything." I smothered a yawn.

"Is that supposed to reassure me?"

"They seem to know their business." Donleavy had called earlier that afternoon to inform me that he'd interviewed Bryce and was ruling him out as a suspect. The sheriff department's current theory was that I'd been hit by a stray bullet. Not that there were typically a lot of bullets flying on the University of Shenandoah campus, but the school had an SCCC chapter. Maybe a member of Students for Concealed Carry on Campus had been aiming at a possum or a cat or some other perceived threat. My own theories hadn't panned out, so that made as much sense as anything. A freak accident. Stranger things had happened to me.

"You're taking this awfully calmly."

I raised a dismissive shoulder. "There's no point in worrying about it." What I didn't tell him was having done my own reconnaissance and come up empty, I wasn't expecting the local sheriff department to do any better. "I'm more nervous about getting through this party tonight."

Stephen gave a fistful of my hair a gentle tug. "It'll all be over in a few hours. And then that's it for the holiday social obligations. When we close the door on the last guest tonight, it's just you and me, kid. From Christmas 'til New Year's Day."

I couldn't pretend it didn't make me happy. "Do you mind?"

"I do not. Not in the least."

I reached to pull him down. His mouth was warm and tasted of cinnamon from the wassail he'd been drinking. When our lips parted he said, "I wish I knew."

"What?"

Stephen smiled, brushed the hair back from my forehead. "It doesn't matter."

"What were you going to say?"

He looked self-conscious for an instant. "I don't know. There's not a lot I can give you."

I sat up. "What are you talking about?"

He laughed at my alarm. "I don't mean it that way. I mean for Christmas. You don't care much about worldly goods. When you do want something, you get it for yourself. You've pretty much been everywhere. There's not much you haven't seen. You're hard to buy for."

I relaxed. “Not in the least. It’s a novelty having someone give me presents. I like anything. Anything you give me, I’ll enjoy.”

“You remember you said that when I give you a hand-crocheted sweater with appliqué penguins.”

“You should give it to me now. I’ll wear it tonight and you can show me off to your posh friends.”

Stephen laughed so loudly he startled Buck awake.

Chapter Five

I hated parties.

This was not to say that I didn't know how to behave at a social event. I'd been to plenty of them, state dinners and *Id al-Kabir,* and never disgraced myself or my government at either. But I was not what one would call a party animal. I couldn't recall any party I'd been to in recent memory that I hadn't been working, one way or the other.

That night was no exception.

I had, as always, a mission. That night my mission was to charm Stephen's friends. To demonstrate to all what an intelligent, pleasant, well-balanced partner Stephen had found for himself. Perhaps a little young, but mature for his age. And what an adorable accent! Stephen didn't care what his friends and colleagues thought of me, but I did—for Stephen's sake.

So I smiled and made small talk and made sure everyone's glass was topped up and that no one was left on their own for too long.

Bryce and his date arrived about an hour and a half into the melee. I didn't recognize the date, a tall, handsome, black man. Bryce introduced us briefly and steered "Kenneth" away from me.

Anne Norton, another doctor at Shenandoah Memorial, tried to persuade me to sample a candy cane martini. Apparently you can get away with any alcoholic atrocity provided you slap the label "martini" on it. I managed to choke down a couple mouthfuls of peppermint and vodka.

"Stephen tells us you used to be in the civil service," one of the old codgers from Stephen's Civil War battlefield preservation committee said. "In my day that was code for spook."

I replied, "In my day it was code for civil servant."

Across the room, I spotted Bryce talking to Stephen. I saw Stephen's gaze slide in my direction. I looked apologetic.

I saw Stephen take a deep breath before focusing on Bryce once more.

"Did you know Stephen's father, the senator?" someone else was asking me.

"No. He died not long after Stephen and I met."

"He was a real character. They don't make them like the Senator anymore."

And so it went. I tried not to look at the clock. Any clock. But as the hours ticked past I felt more and more cheerful. Soon we would close the door, turn off the porch light, and it would be just me and Stephen. The best Christmas present in the world.

Shortly before midnight I noticed the wood basket was empty. I grabbed my waxed coat from the mud porch and went out to collect more firewood.

A few flakes of white drifted desultorily down. The night smelled cold and clean, of snow and wood smoke. The full moon was sinking beneath the black tree tops but it cast bright radiance across the white blanketed yard. The lake was frozen and still, the geese gone for the winter. Music and laughter drifted from the house as I made my way to the neatly stacked woodpile.

As I rounded the corner of the house, a slim shadow detached itself from the siding. A woman. I had an impression of large shining eyes, long dark hair, a dark wool cap, a dark wool coat.

"Getting a breath of fresh air?" I said.

She didn't answer immediately and I knew. The hair on the back of my neck rose in belated recognition. My survival instincts were not what they had once been. Too late, too slow.

She pointed a revolver at me. It gleamed in the moonlight. Too big for her small hands.

There was nowhere for me to go. Nowhere to run and nothing to use as a shield.

"I knew you would come out tonight," she said. She sounded young. Younger than me anyway. "Somehow I knew."

"Do I know you?"

"Don't you?" She spoke English well, but she had an accent. Indo European. Afghanistan. Dari or Pashto?

"Not a friend, I'm guessing."

"No. I'm not your friend." She was careful to stay in the deep shade of the building, to stay out of reach. "I tried to shoot you the other night."

"Was it something I said?" I kept my eyes on her hands and the revolver. She was not comfortable with firearms, but she did appear to know the basics. And the basics were all it took.

She said breathlessly, "It's something you did. Something you did to me and my family."

It was a good sign we were talking. A good sign she hadn't shot me on sight. I said, "I'm sorry."

"No you're not. You don't even remember me." She took a deep, sharp breath. "I lost my nerve the last time. The gun was louder than I expected." She glanced down at the weapon she held and at once—before I could move—back up at me.

"Why don't you tell me what it is I did to you?"

The pale blur of her face twisted. "Do you remember Hamid Farnood? Dr. Hamid Farnood?"

Vaguely. "Yes," I said. It had been at least ten years ago. One of those things I'd blocked out the best I could. No point brooding over what couldn't be changed.

"You remember you betrayed him? Tricked him? Killed him?" Her hands shook and I braced for the shot. It didn't come.

"I don't remember that." It was coming back to me, though. One of my earliest jobs in Afghanistan. Not my finest hour. Not the finest hour of any of us. Farnood was a respected cardiologist who had for a patient a particular al-Qaeda lieutenant that my section was intent on taking out. Farnood was our best way in. He was a progressive and a western sympathizer, but his *kafir* tendencies were tolerated because of his skill as a doctor.

"Because of you, my father was executed."

"Anoosheh," I said slowly. I remembered her now. A gawky schoolgirl with big eyes and a little-kid giggle. Smart and shy. She had adored her father. And—painful to remember—she'd developed a crush on me those summer weeks while we'd worked with her father to put our plans into action.

"Anoosheh. Yes. *Now* you remember."

"I'm sorry," I said. "I didn't know." I could have guessed though. By the time we'd pulled the plug on the operation, moved our sights to another target, it was too late for Farnood. We left him exposed. He'd stretched too far, shown his hand. His fate was sealed, inevitable. I believe I'd objected, argued, but not very hard or for very long. In the end I had coped, as I had learned to cope with many such situations, by not allowing myself to think of it.

And now it seemed my turn, my fate sealed, inevitable.

I heard the quiet bang of the back porch door, and I knew with terrified instinct who it was.

"Let's go down to the pond," I told Anoosheh. "We can talk there. You don't want any interruptions."

She shrank back against the house. "You think you'll overpower me and throw my body in the lake."

I'd thought it was a possibility, yes, but somehow watching her draw back, hearing the fear in her voice, I knew I wouldn't be able to carry through. I couldn't stop seeing her as that skinny, giggling girl with the solemn eyes.

"I just want to talk to you."

"Mark?" Stephen called.

I called back, "Coming. I'll be right in!" I never turned my gaze from Anoosheh and she never moved. I could hear the quick sound of her breaths.

But Stephen's footsteps continued forward, that sliding smoosh of snow underfoot. "You've been awhile," he said.

"Stephen, you don't need to—" But it was too late. He rounded the corner and stopped in his tracks.

I thought she would panic then and shoot one of us. Her fear was a tangible thing. But somehow she controlled it.

"What's going on?" Stephen said calmly, though I'm sure he had a pretty good idea.

"Just chatting with an old friend," I said. "Go back and get warm inside."

"Who's your friend?" Stephen asked at the same moment Annoosheh said, "No!"

I said to her, "Be smart. This is not a complication you need or want."

"But now he's here. The doctor. Doctor Thorpe."

"And you are?" Stephen asked.

I said tersely, "Someone I used to know."

"My name is Anoosheh Farnood. Your…lover killed my father. Destroyed my family."

To my horror, Stephen put his hand on my shoulder and calmly, coolly moved between me and Anoosheh. "And you think…what? That shooting Mark is going to make things right?"

"What the hell are you doing?" I said to him. I tried to keep my own voice quiet, reasonable. I didn't dare struggle with him or make any quick moves for fear of sparking Anoosheh into action.

"What did he do?" Stephen asked her. I knew that voice so well, deep and unworried, and infinitely kind. I'd never known anyone fail to respond to it, and Anoosheh was no different. The story poured out of her, as much as she knew of it. Enough. She knew enough.

"And then when I saw him on campus. I couldn't believe it was him. But it *was* him. I followed him a couple of times. Sat near him in the library. He never recognized me. He had forgotten me. Forgotten all of it."

"I haven't forgotten."

She ignored me. "My father died and *he* went on living. He was happy and my life was destroyed."

"I'm sorry," Stephen said. "No one should have to live through such things.

"No! They shouldn't!"

"You're a brave young woman. A resilient young lady. And now you're living with your aunt and uncle?"

"Yes." Anoosheh was crying. I wasn't sure if that was a good sign or not. She kept that cannon trained right on Stephen's midsection. He had a longer reach than me, but she kept her distance.

"And if you do this thing, shoot the both of us with your uncle's gun, what do you think that will do to these people who love you so much?"

"I—" Her voice broke.

"You say Mark destroyed your family, destroyed you, but you're not destroyed. Look at what you've done already. You came to this country and you're going to school and making your aunt and uncle proud."

Anoosheh said fiercely, "Only *him*. I'll only kill *him*!"

Stephen sounded kind, "No. You'll have to shoot me too, because I won't let you hurt him while I can stop you. I don't think you'd get far, but even if you did get away from here, you wouldn't get over this. *This* would destroy you, and it would destroy the people you love."

I made another effort to shove in front of Stephen but he blocked me with his shoulder. I didn't dare struggle with him. Didn't dare give her a reason to fire.

"He killed my father!"

"The men who shot your father killed him. I know the job Mark did and the way he worked. He'd have presented a choice for your father, and your father, being the kind of man he obviously was, chose to risk his life for his country and for his family. Because he'd want something better for you."

"No! They tricked him. *He* tricked him."

Stephen didn't let up, quiet, relentless. "You say your father was a doctor. I didn't have the privilege of knowing him, but I know he wouldn't want to see you, his beloved daughter, standing here now with a gun in your hand."

Anoosheh began to sob. Her head bowed, the revolver fell to the snow. Sounds of grief tore from her. Stephen stepped forward, took her in his arms, and held her while she cried.

* * * * *

It was very late—in fact, technically Christmas—by the time the last guest climbed into a taxi and trundled away, down the snowy lane. The caterers finishing clearing up, packed their wares, and left.

Stephen and I sat in front of the fire having a nightcap. The only light in the room came from the flames and the colored lights on the tree.

Stephen's arm stretched along the top of the sofa. His fingers played idly with the ends of my hair, sending little frissons feathering up and down my spine. "Are you upset that I didn't want to call the police?"

"You're joking I assume?"

He shook his head.

"No. I'm not upset. I don't regard the girl an ongoing threat."

He smiled faintly. "Are you genuinely this dispassionate about it?"

"I wasn't remotely dispassionate out there. Not when you walked outside." I swallowed. "Don't ever do that again, will you? Don't ever walk between me and someone holding a weapon."

The hint of humor was still in his voice. "It's not something I plan to make a habit of."

For a moment the firelight and the glitter of the brandy in our glasses and the twinkling amidst the tree branches were all too bright. I closed my eyes. My throat felt tight. I hoped Anoosheh was the last of my ghosts. What if she wasn't?

"Mark?"

"Mm?"

"Let it go."

I opened my eyes, turned my head. Stephen's eyes were two more shining points of light in the gloom.

"Of course."

"I'm serious," Stephen said. He sounded serious. "Dickens said it. Stay in the sunlight. Don't look for trouble that might never happen."

"Dickens never said that. Dickens never thought that."

"Maybe it was Ben Franklin."

I laughed a shaky laugh.

We were quiet for a time. Then Stephen said, "Would you like to open a couple of your Christmas presents?"

"All right."

He rose, went behind the sofa to the tree and came back with a couple of parcels. He handed me the largest first. A large box wrapped in silver paper decorated with snowflakes.

I smoothed the paper. I felt absurdly moved to be sitting here, together. Not just to be alive—though I was certainly grateful for that—but to have love as well. What other gift could compare with that?

I opened the box, pulled aside the tissue. A brown leather jacket. Very similar to the one that had been destroyed. I smiled at Stephen. "Thank you. I like it very much."

"Let's agree to no bullet holes in this one."

"Agreed."

I opened the second smaller parcel. It was a book bound in leather that looked the color of blood in the firelight. I read the gilt letters embossed on the distressed face. "*The Christmas Cake.*"

"Since you weren't able to buy the original."

"How did you manage this?"

"It wasn't difficult," Stephen said wryly.

"It wasn't? I had no idea it was going to be published."

A lost Dickens manuscript, a Christmas story, had resurfaced the previous year. I and every other Dickens collector across the galaxy had tried to obtain it, but in the end the owner had decided not to sell.

"No? Well, there's a romantic story behind the decision to publish the manuscript."

I opened the book. In the wavering light I could just make out the first line. *Our story begins with a fallen star. But the star is not the story.*

I looked up, smiling. "Oh yes?"

"The owner, who turns out to be gay—"

"Really?"

"It happens, so I hear. He went to Los Angeles to sell the book and apparently met the love of his life. So he gave his new lover the book."

"Sweet."

"And the man was a book collector so naturally he couldn't bear to part with it. Except the sale of the book was supposed to finance a special school the original owner had been dreaming of building. So the new owner hit on the idea of having the book published as a limited Christmas edition." Stephen nodded to the book. "It's an exact replica of the original."

"Brilliant. I can't wait to read it. I hope it pays off for them."

"I imagine they'll make a fortune."

"I have something special for you, too."

Stephen raised his eyebrows, his expression droll.

"Close. But no. That comes next." I rose and went round to the tree and found the package I wanted.

Stephen unwrapped the small box and held up the plane tickets. "Montreal?"

“Paris without the jet lag. You’ve never been there and neither have I. I thought we could explore it together.”

“I thought you wanted to stay home for the holidays?”

“That’s not your idea of the holidays. And all I really wanted was for us to have time together. Alone.”

Stephen’s smile was quizzical. “So you decided to fly us to a foreign metropolis for New Year’s?”

“There’s no place more alone than a big city where you don’t know anyone. Anyone except the bloke you’re with.”

He glanced at the tickets and then back at me. “Are you sure about this? I wanted our first Christmas to be exactly what you wanted.”

I leaned forward to kiss him. “It is.”

Acknowledgements

Sincere thanks — and happiest of holidays — to Susan Sorrentino, Andrea Slayde, Pender Mackie, Hambel, Stella, Caroline Davies and—always—Janet.

About the Author

A distinct voice in gay fiction, multi-award-winning author JOSH LANYON has been writing gay mystery, adventure and romance for over a decade. In addition to numerous short stories, novellas, and novels, Josh is the author of the critically acclaimed Adrien English series, including The Hell You Say, winner of the 2006 USABookNews awards for GLBT Fiction. Josh is an Eppie Award winner and a three-time Lambda Literary Award finalist.

Find other Josh Lanyon titles at www.joshlanyon.com

Made in the USA
Lexington, KY
28 December 2012